# BARBARY

# BARBARY

## Vonda N. McIntyre

Houghton Mifflin Company
Boston 1986

*Fic.
Mc Int*

B +T 7.94 (12, 70)
3/16/87

Library of Congress Cataloging-in-Publication Data

McIntyre, Vonda N.
Barbary.

Summary: Orphaned Barbary finds a new home on a space station but runs into difficulties trying to protect her pet cat Mickey.
[1. Science fiction.  2. Orphans—Fiction.
3. Cats—Fiction]  I. Title.
PZ7.M478656Bar  1986      [Fic]      86-9766
ISBN 0-395-41029-0

Chapter Eight appeared in the
Spring Issue of *The Seattle Review.*

Printed in the United States of America

S 10 9 8 7 6 5 4 3 2 1

I'm grateful to Dr. John G. Cramer, of the University of Washington in Seattle. He offered expert advice that helped immeasurably in the creation of the research station *Einstein* and, particularly, in the descriptions of what it would feel like to live and work in an environment in which gravity is provided by radial acceleration.

I'm also indebted to Dr. Gerard K. O'Neill, of Princeton, the Geostar Corporation, and the Space Studies Institute (Box 82, Princeton, NJ 08540). The society to which Barbary emigrates grew out of Dr. O'Neill's proposals for permanent inhabited orbiting colonies, the mass driver, and other practical ideas for allowing human beings to live in space.

V.N.M.

For my other sister

# BARBARY

# Chapter One

High in the corners of the spaceport waiting room, four small TV screens displayed a space shuttle, piggybacked on external fuel tanks, shedding clouds of vapor down its flanks.

Barbary watched the shuttle intently. Other times she might have wished to see it real, instead of filtered through lenses and electronics. Other times, but not now.

She brushed her fingertips across the front of her baggy jacket, checking for her ticket in one of its many outside pockets. She had buttoned the ticket safely in; she knew she had not lost it. During her first hours in the waiting room, two weeks ago, she had made touching the ticket a habit. The habit no longer reassured her, though, for she had been bumped off two flights and the ticket had been revalidated twice. Now, as launch approached, she felt the awful certainty that once more she would not get on board.

She fumbled in another pocket of the jacket, pulled out her old silver dollar, and passed it across the knuckles of her right hand. She flipped it over and over with her fingers,

1

caught it with her thumb, brought it under her palm and back up onto her knuckles, then started over again. The trick was a good one to do when she felt nervous, because it took a lot of concentration.

The antique coin slipped from her fingers and bounced on the carpet. She scooped it up, clutched it, and shoved it deep into her pocket. The worn edges dug into her palm. She was not very good at sleight of hand. She had only begun to learn it, or any other sort of stage magic, three months before. Doing it well took years of practice.

She knew it took years; she knew she was not very good. She just hoped she was good enough.

She touched her ticket once more, feeling the hard edge of plastic beneath the rough material of the army surplus jacket. She forced herself to keep her hand away from the single pocket inside her jacket, the secret pocket, to think about anything except the weight pressing against her side. It was important to pretend the secret pocket carried nothing, important to believe the secret pocket did not even exist. If she believed nothing was there, no one else would suspect. But if anyone found out, she would never ride the shuttle even if a place opened up for her.

So far, fifty-four passengers had boarded. Barbary had been here since before they began loading and she had counted every one of them. She knew they were all important, and she recognized many of them from the news. No one would say whether they were going to the low-earth-orbit space station, or farther out to the O'Neill colonies, where human beings lived permanently, or even all the way to the research station, *Einstein*, where Barbary was supposed to be going. No one would even say why they were leaving earth. No one had to say that whatever they were doing and wherever they were going, they were much more important than one twelve-year-old emigrant.

Still, only fifty-four had boarded, and the ship, in this configuration, could carry sixty. She might finally have a chance for a place. She wished she knew. Her social worker, Mr. Smith, had gone to check the reservations again.

Barbary slumped back in the uncomfortable waiting room seat. Her feet did not reach the floor, and the arms of the chair rose too high for her to sit cross-legged.

The door opened. Barbary glanced around, expecting Mr. Smith. Instead, a frail and elderly Native American entered, accompanied by one of the port attendants. By now Barbary knew most of the attendants by name. This one was Jack. He treated the new passenger with great deference. Though she spoke too softly for Barbary to make out her words, Barbary could feel her presence, her aura of calm and quiet power.

Barbary suddenly realized why she looked familiar. Like so many of the passengers who had already boarded, she, too, frequently appeared on the news. Ambassador Begay represented the United Tribes of North America at the United Nations. A year before, she had been elected United Nations secretary-general.

She preceded Jack into the loading tunnel and disappeared.

Though all the space colonies sent ambassadors to the

United Nations, Barbary had never heard of a secretary-general visiting a colony before, or even going into space. Barbary read news about the colonies and the research station whenever she could find it. She was sure she would have remembered if they had received a United Nations mission. Even if they had, this trip should have gotten some attention. Particularly during the last month, Barbary had had very little to do but watch TV, and read, and wait, either at the juvenile home or here at the spaceport. The secretary-general's trip had gone unreported. With Ambassador Begay and all the other famous people on board the shuttle, reporters and cameras ought to be swarming all over the place. Instead, the port was practically deserted.

Something secret, something unusual, was going on, something to do with the space colonies.

Barbary wondered angrily what the big mystery was. Any other time she would have been fascinated and curious, but right now what mattered was that she would probably be bumped off this flight, too. If she did not take today's shuttle, the space transport would boost from low earth orbit to the research station, *Einstein*, without her. *Einstein* traveled in a highly elliptical polar orbit that took it far from earth, even farther than the moon. For three-quarters of its orbit, it lay out of range of any spacecraft. If she did not catch this evening's transport, she would have to wait over a month for the next trip. And a month from now would be too late.

Her fear made her angry and defensive. This was a matter of life and death.

She forced herself not to reach into the secret pocket to be sure everything was all right.

It isn't there, she thought. Don't touch it. Nothing's in it. It isn't even there.

And so what if I don't get on board this time, or ever? she thought, trying to persuade herself not to care. It probably won't make any difference at all. Even if I get to go to space, everything will probably be just the same.

Jack came out of the loading tunnel and strode across the waiting room, ignoring Barbary.

"When do I get to go on board?" she asked. In the silence of the small room, her voice sounded loud and sullen.

I don't care if I get to go or not, she thought. I really don't care.

She tried to make herself believe it.

Jack stopped and turned unwillingly toward her, tired of answering her questions.

"Look, I just don't know, all right?" He made himself grin. "Why don't you go get yourself a nice glass of juice?"

Though her stomach had been growling for the past hour, Barbary shook her head. That was a clincher. The instructions for riding the shuttle recommended eating a light breakfast, and nothing afterward. If Jack thought Barbary had a chance to get on board today, he would not tell her to drink anything. She wished he would just say so and be done with it, instead of patronizing her with fake smiles.

Turning away from him, trying to hold back tears, she glared at the closed-circuit TV. Watching it was like being in a dream where she could see herself from a distance, for the waiting room in which she sat was quite visible as a low concrete building near the launch tower. Nothing moved in the picture except the long wisps of vapor.

When Jack returned, he accompanied three people in business suits. One carried a briefcase. He was middle-aged, and though Barbary could not immediately place him, he looked as familiar as the secretary-general. The other two were much younger, and they were obviously his body-guards. Both wore half-tinted glasses, the kind that would darken in sunlight. One wore an earring — an earphone, like a TV reporter's — and the other wore a wide, thin bracelet, a nanocomputer, the smallest Barbary had ever seen.

None of them spoke. The first bodyguard went ahead into the tunnel. Jack stood aside for the others to precede him, but the second bodyguard motioned him on with a quick jerk of his head, waited for Jack and the older man to pass, then brought up the rear. Barbary watched the silent ballet. Under other circumstances she might have laughed. But nothing felt very funny right now. Jack returned, looking grim.

"Who were they?" Barbary said.

"Never mind."

"You might as well tell me, I'm going to remember for myself in a minute. The old guy, anyway."

Jack shrugged. "You'll have to, then, because I can't tell you. You probably shouldn't even be here to see him."

"I have a right to be here! I have a ticket. I have a reservation. Just like I did twice before!"

6

"Look, there isn't anything I can do."

Barbary remembered. "The guy who wasn't wired up was the vice president," she said. "That's right, isn't it? Those bodyguards are coming back out, aren't they?"

"No."

"You mean he's taking them to the research station? Why? What for?"

"Rules. Federal law, for all I know."

"He's taking up two extra seats," Barbary said, then stopped her pointless protest. Jack knew as well as she did — as well as anybody who knew anything did — how useless bodyguards would be in space. No one owned weapons; everyone in the small population knew everyone else. The crime rate was so low that there practically was no crime rate. Barbary supposed that people sometimes got mad enough to want to punch each other out, and maybe even did it once in a while, but the deliberate, vicious sort of violence that made bodyguards necessary on earth simply never happened.

"Bodyguards," Barbary said with disgust.

Jack shrugged. No doubt he had to face stupid rules even more often than Barbary did. They were not his fault. That was the trouble. They were never anybody's fault. Therefore no one could ever be found who had the authority to bend or break or stretch them.

"Nothing I can do," Jack said, and left the waiting room.

Barbary rose and walked to the tunnel, lugging her duffel bag. She hesitated at the entrance, then plunged inside. The weight of the secret pocket bumped gently against her side. She kept herself from looking down to see if the lump showed. She knew it did not. Even if it did, it was too late now.

She got as far as the elevator. She had hoped that the one attendant took passengers all the way to their seats, and that she could get on board in between Jack's trips. Trying to stow away on a spaceship would be dumb, apart from being dangerous and probably impossible, but Barbary had a ticket for her seat and she hoped that maybe, just maybe, if she got inside, they would let her stay rather than making all the fuss of putting her off.

But another spaceport employee waited at the elevator. Barbary pulled out her ticket and offered it up. The agent took it, slid it through the sensor, and nodded at the read-out.

"Your ticket's all right," she said, "but where's Jack?"

"He said to go on," Barbary said.

"He's supposed to bring you himself."

Barbary shrugged as pleasantly as she could. Since she had no idea what emergency might call Jack away, it made a lot more sense for her not to try to make one up. "He said just come on."

The agent touched a key on the sensor and glanced at the read-out again. "There are still three people ahead of you on the reservation list, and only two seats. There isn't any change there."

Barbary held herself back from snapping "I've been bumped twice already," and said instead, "He said to get on board."

She heard footsteps behind her. She had lost her gamble.

8

The footsteps stopped. Jack cleared his throat. With her shoulders slumped, Barbary turned around.

The passenger accompanying Jack would take up the next to last seat. Barbary glared at her, but her anger changed to astonishment when she recognized the astronaut Jeanne Velory. The tall Black woman carried a scuffed briefcase and a small backpack. Her short curly hair was so dark it sparkled, and her eyes were deep green, the color of a pine forest. She was even more striking than photographs and news tapes hinted. She gazed down quizzically.

Jack frowned. "Go back to the waiting room and sit down," he said with some asperity. "Or go home and wait for the next liftoff."

Humiliated and furious, fighting tears again, Barbary pushed past him. She refused to cry, and she refused to leave. In the waiting room she flung herself into a chair and tried to think.

"Barbary . . ."

She started. She had not heard Mr. Smith come back in. The social worker stood over her, looking down with his perpetually sad expression. He never acted happy or excited about anything. Only sad.

"We might as well go. I'm afraid you're not going to get on this flight, either."

"There's one more seat."

"I know. But it's reserved. In fact it's reserved for two different people, and they don't know what to do about that."

"Kick both the others off and give me the place. It's mine! It isn't fair!"

9

"Perhaps not," he said. "But there's a meeting at the station. They have to transport the participants."

"And they figure somebody who's only twelve years old doesn't have anything better to do, anyway, except sit here waiting."

He blinked his sad brown eyes. "If you want to look at it that way, I'm afraid that's quite true. But I'd advise you to accept the delay gracefully. You've caused us all considerable worry, with your stubbornness and your running away."

"I didn't run away!" Barbary said. "I had to find a new home for Mickey!" If he stopped believing what she had told him, everything was ruined.

"You risked your emigrant status. You should have sent that cat to the pound."

"You —!"

She stopped herself in time. She wanted to swear at him, to scream and curse. She could do it, too. She knew words he had probably never heard of, and she knew how to use them. Up to a couple of months ago, she would have. But Barbary had recently noticed that civilized people did not swear, and that they looked down on people who did. If she wanted to live on the research station, if she wanted her new family to let her stay and to have some regard for her, she had to learn to behave like a civilized person.

Instead of cussing Mr. Smith out, she glared at him and turned her back.

"I know you're eager to get to your new home," Mr. Smith said. "But you ought to look on the delay as an opportunity. You might not be back on earth for years. You have a chance to look at things for the last time, and see things you've never seen before —"

"There's nothing I want to see again and nothing I want to see for the first time, not here. I want to leave and I don't care if I never come back!"

He hesitated, as if shocked by her determination. "Well," he said, "all right. But you aren't going to be able to leave today. Let's go home." He took her wrist.

Barbary twisted her hand from his grasp. "I'm staying right here till they let me on or lift off without me. And if they go without me I may stay here anyhow!"

On the TV screen, the shuttle prepared to launch. It had to take off within a specific period of time, during the launch window. When those few minutes had passed and the shuttle lifted off, Barbary's last chance would vanish in the trail of the rockets.

Jack came out of the tunnel. He walked through the waiting room quickly, without looking at Barbary.

"There's one seat left," she said as he reached the door.

He stood very still with his shoulders hunched and stiff. After a moment he faced her

"Now, see here —" He cut off the words and began again, though he still sounded angry. "You aren't going to get on this flight."

"Kick off those bodyguards. Then there'll be room for everybody."

"I can't do that."

"The ship can't wait much longer," Barbary said with desperation. "We're already into the launch window. Let me get on. Tell the pilot to take off and tell the people who're coming that they're too late. Everybody knows you can't delay a shuttle like any old airplane. Then you won't have to try to figure out which one of them to give the seat to."

Jack not only looked tempted, he looked as if he were about to grin. But he shook his head. "I don't have the authority."

"Then who does?" Barbary cried.

He left the room, not even looking back.

"Barbary, please sit down," Mr. Smith said. "Relax. I can't understand why you're so upset. Be reasonable. It isn't going to hurt you to wait for the next shuttle."

"Yes it is! I have to —!" She stopped, afraid she had already said too much, afraid she had aroused his suspicions. She was on her feet, clutching her silver coin till its smooth-worn edge cut into her palm. She did not even remember standing up. Holding back tears of rage and frustration, she obeyed Mr. Smith's request. She did not know what she was going to do if she had to wait for another liftoff. She feared she would have to choose between abandoning her chance to emigrate and breaking a promise that meant as much to her as her dreams.

# Chapter Two

The seconds display on the clock flicked along as if time were speeding up. Neither of the other two passengers had arrived.

"They can't leave without me," Barbary said.

"I'm afraid they can," Mr. Smith said. "So let's go home."

"But I'm right here, and they're taking off with an empty place."

"There's nothing to be done about it, Barbary. These things happen. Come along, now."

He took her arm. She jumped up and tried to pull away.

"It's stupid!" she said. "It doesn't make any sense! It's — it's a waste of taxpayers' money!" Even as she said it she knew how ridiculous it sounded, though it was perfectly true.

"You're right," someone behind her said.

Mr. Smith looked up. Startled, Barbary turned.

Jeanne Velory stood in the entrance tunnel, leaning out with her hands against its sides.

"You're right," she said again to Barbary. "Come on, let's go."

Mr. Smith was so surprised that his grip on Barbary's arm loosened. She pulled away. Dr. Velory grinned and disappeared into the tunnel. Barbary grabbed her duffel bag and sprinted after her, without a backward look.

She had to run to keep up. The secret pocket jounced. She bent slightly sideways to try to hold it still.

At the elevator, Dr. Velory stopped and waited, holding the door for her. "Are you okay? Do you have a stitch in your side?"

"No," Barbary said, then, "well, yeah, I guess."

Dr. Velory let the doors close. The elevator lifted them past several rows of seats, then stopped. Doors on each side opened. The vice president and one of his bodyguards sat on the left. The vice president read a newspaper and the bodyguard watched for assassins.

Dr. Velory gestured to the right, to the last empty seats. Because the shuttle had to sit on its tail for liftoff, the place that would have been the floor in a regular airplane formed a vertical surface, like a wall leading up between the passenger seats, which lay flat back in the horizontal position necessary for liftoff.

Barbary slid across and into her place. The elevator fell away, then its shaft retracted. It was part of the launch facility, not part of the spacecraft. After delivering the passengers to their places, it withdrew behind the safety of walls of concrete. The doors of the shuttle bay closed, sealing the passengers safely inside.

Barbary looked around. One of the bodyguards watched her from across the aisle.

"That was pretty risky, Dr. Velory."

"Not nearly as risky as having Reston and Kartoff arguing over one seat," she said.

Instead of responding to her joke, he frowned. "Just what we need right now on the station — a kid."

"She'll be a good deal less out of place," Dr. Velory said, her voice soft and cool, "than the Secret Service."

The vice president remained hidden behind his newspaper as the bodyguard started to retort.

The second bodyguard leaned toward them from the next row down. "Why don't you lighten up, Frank?"

Frank glared at him, too, then snorted in annoyance and lay back in his seat with his arms folded.

Dr. Velory reached over and strapped Barbary in. Barbary had to squirm to keep the secret pocket free of the harness. She could see the bulge, but she hoped all the outside pockets would conceal it from everyone else.

"That's a terrific jacket," Dr. Velory said to Barbary.

Barbary felt the blood rising to her cheeks, in embarrassment and fear of being found out. "Thanks," she said.

"You won't really need it on the station, but I can see why you like it."

Barbary was too flustered to say anything.

"What's your name?"

"Barbary."

15

"I'm Jeanne."

"I know," Barbary said hesitantly. "Thanks. For getting me on board."

"It was self-preservation. Reston and Kartoff are always competing, and I'm right next to the ecological niche they both would have wanted."

The ship vibrated all around them.

"Are we starting?"

"Not quite yet. A few more minutes. It's easiest if you can relax — I know that sounds hard."

"How many times have you gone into space?"

"Oh, goodness, I don't know. I've lost track. A couple of dozen, I suppose."

But on one of her trips into space she commanded the *Ares* mission, the mission that sent people to Mars. The year *Ares* launched itself from low earth orbit, Barbary was only six, so she barely remembered it. But she remembered very clearly when it came back three years later. The *Ares* astronauts returned with samples of Martian life, the organisms that all the robot missions had missed.

"Are you emigrating to one of the O'Neill colonies?"

"No," Barbary said. She had never before felt in awe of anyone she had actually met. But the scientist sitting beside her had been, with her shipmates, farther from earth than anyone else in the world. She had walked on another planet, not just the moon, but Mars.

"No," Barbary said again, embarrassed that her voice sounded shaky. "I'm going to the same place you are, to *Einstein*, to the research station." But I'm just going there to live, she thought. Not to be in charge of everything.

16

"Oh," Jeanne said. "You'll be a member of our interesting little tour group, then."

"They're *all* going to *Einstein?* For a tour? If that s the only reason, why weren't there any cameras or reporters when they left?"

Jeanne gazed at her for several moments without answering. She was silent for so long that Barbary wondered if she had said something wrong.

"You might as well know now," Jeanne said. "Everybody off earth already does. We're a greeting party, I think. I hope. Maybe an archeological expedition. Something entered the solar system about a year ago. At first we thought it was just a comet. But it isn't. It's an alien ship."

"An alien ship!" Barbary thought of three questions all at the same time. "Who — where — how come nobody's told us about them?"

Jeanne smiled. "We don't know where they're from, and I agree that it's dumb for it to be kept a secret. The council thinks everybody will be frightened, and maybe that's true. But they're going to have to know sooner or later. I go along with the people who think sooner would be better, so we'd all have time to get used to the idea."

"What do they look like?"

Jeanne shrugged. "We don't know. They haven't responded to any of our radio transmissions. They aren't transmitting in any mode we know how to detect. Maybe they aren't ready to talk to us or show themselves to us yet. Maybe they're waiting to see how we react to their ship. Or maybe there isn't anybody on board. A lot of people think the ship's a derelict. I don't believe it, myself. But it *could*

17

have been floating around in the universe for millions of years, with nobody left inside. That's part of the trouble with announcing that it's there — I've just told you about all there is to tell about it. People will want to know more. I sure do."

"Are you going out to it?"

"If I can persuade the council to send a ship," Jeanne said, "you can bet I'll be on it."

The faint vibrations of the shuttle increased.

"Remember what I told you about liftoff," Jeanne said. "Relax. Take slow deep breaths, then exhale slowly."

Barbary inched her hand sideways till it lay over the secret pocket. Then she realized how much her hand would weigh when the acceleration reached its height, so she jerked her fingers away again.

The sound increased suddenly.

The shuttle lifted off.

Acceleration pressed Barbary into her seat.

Barbary had dreamed of riding the shuttle since she first realized that people were inside that little ship attached to its ungainly fuel tanks, blasting away so beautifully and with such speed and power. She had read every description of space travel that she could find; she had imagined how this would be. But she had not imagined enough.

She wanted to laugh, she wanted to cry. Then all her thoughts were overwhelmed by the liftoff, the acceleration, the incredible noise. Though the forces of acceleration pressing her down did not hurt, it seemed as though she could count each individual lock of hair clamped between

18

the seat back and her scalp, as though she could feel each ridge of her fingerprints pressed against the armrests.

Suddenly the acceleration and the sound stopped and she felt completely weightless: she took a moment to realize that she really was in zero gravity, not simply relieved of the extra weight of acceleration. Before she could move, the second set of fuel tanks ignited.

The brief instant of weightlessness blended with the acceleration. One seemed hardly any different from the other, they were both so strange to her.

The vibration and noise of the engines cut off. In the intense quiet, Barbary could hardly tell if the sound in her ears was her heartbeat or the echo of the rocket. She lay very still.

She was in space.

"Feel all right?"

"Yes, I . . ." Barbary said, then stopped, uncertain. This time weightlessness was more than a lurch and an instant's change. She had thought she knew what to expect: "A long ride down in a fast elevator," someone had written. But it was more than that; and it continued. Barbary wondered if anyone *could* describe it. She would have plenty of time to try. From now on, where she intended to live, gravity would be the artificial condition and free fall the natural one.

"Are you sure?" Jeanne sounded worried.

"I had to decide," Barbary said. "Yes. I like it. It's great."

Jeanne grinned. "Good."

Once the ship reached orbit, the couches no longer lay horizontal. The floor no longer extended up and down like a wall, but it did not lie "beneath" Barbary, either. There was no "up" or "down," no "beneath" or "above." Barbary found that depending on how she looked at anything she could give it a different orientation, as if she were inside a tremendous optical illusion.

"It all takes a while to get used to," Jeanne said. "Excuse me a minute — I want to introduce myself to someone." She unfastened her harness and pushed herself into the aisle. Free and graceful, she drifted a few seats ahead and paused beside Ambassador Begay. She said something in a language Barbary had never heard. The elderly diplomat glanced up at Jeanne, startled, then smiled and replied in what must have been the same language. She extended her hand, and Jeanne shook it gently. They talked for a few more minutes, then Jeanne smiled and nodded and with one easy push floated back to Barbary.

"I always wanted to meet her," Jeanne said. "I hope there's time to talk to her some more, up on the station."

Barbary realized, with surprise, that Jeanne felt as much admiration for the secretary-general as Barbary did for Jeanne.

"What language was that?" Barbary asked.

"Navaho. It was a requirement in grad school. It's so different from English, particularly in the way it deals with time, that it helps you understand advanced physics. I'm afraid my accent is pretty terrible, though. Say, Barbary, would you like to get up?"

"Sure!" Barbary said, then almost took it back because of the secret pocket. But she could slip out of her jacket and leave it tucked under the harness. Ever since she could remember, she had dreamed of floating in zero gravity, of flying, of freedom.

"Do you think that's a good idea?" Frank, the bodyguard, had only been pretending to ignore them.

"Yes," Jeanne said, ignoring the sarcasm. "I do."

Jeanne freed the catches of Barbary's harness. Barbary drifted away from the comforting solidity of the seat. She glanced back to be sure she had pushed the sleeves of her jacket between the cushion and the arm rests. The action of turning produced a reaction that sent her tumbling, out of reach of anything. Laughing, Jeanne caught her.

"Slowly," she said. "Everything slowly and gently. That's the thing to remember, at least till you get used to it. Then you're less likely to make a mistake, and even if you do, you have time to correct it before you fly across the room and run into a wall."

"Let me try again."

Jeanne drew her to a handhold, let go, and floated backward a few meters along the aisle.

"Push off toward me."

Jeanne did not seem to mind being watched by the other passengers. Most of them looked on with interest, though Frank glowered.

Barbary kicked off toward Jeanne — wrong again: much too hard, much too fast. She flew across the compartment, soaring past the other passengers. Jeanne caught her again. Barbary felt embarrassed.

"It takes a while to get the hang of it," Jeanne said. "Can you swim?"

"Yeah, sort of."

"You can get around that way, though not very fast." She backstroked down the aisle, but with both arms moving together, instead of alternately.

Barbary began to be able to make the direction she decided was "down" stay where she put it, in her mind. But if she thought about her surroundings in a slightly different way, suddenly she would lose "down" and feel as though she was diving scarily toward a floor. It was easier, she found, to think of all the surfaces as walls.

"One more time," Jeanne said, turning toward her.

Barbary steadied herself, aware of everyone watching her. The friendlier bodyguard watched with curiosity, maybe even with some envy. Barbary wondered if he had ever been in space before.

Then suddenly Barbary saw her jacket drifting free above her seat. She leaped to catch it. She arched across the cabin. People shouted and ducked. Her shoulder hit the wall. She bounced back, tumbling. Flailing to regain her balance, she cartwheeled across the compartment. She heard a shouted warning. The toe of her shoe caught the vice president's newspaper and tore it from his hands. With a rattling, ripping sound it wrapped itself around her legs. The second bodyguard tried to catch her, but she was moving too fast. She hit the wall with her other shoulder and rebounded. For a moment she looked straight into the surprised face of the vice president, who still held one shred of newspaper in each hand. She spun away. The face of the second bodyguard flashed by. He had crinkly lines around his eyes as if he were struggling not to laugh.

22

Jeanne, braced against the wall with her foot hooked through a handhold, caught Barbary and held her. As soon as she had stopped, the shuttle started to spin around her and for the first time she felt nauseated. She closed her eyes. Both her shoulders ached. To her surprise, she had managed to grab her jacket and keep hold of it. She clutched it tight.

"I told you this was a mistake!" Frank snarled.

Jeanne ignored him. "Barbary, are you okay? You took a couple of nasty bumps."

"Yeah," Barbary said. The shakiness of her voice surprised her. "I think so." She opened her eyes. Things had stopped spinning. "That was dumb," she said. "That was really dumb." She glanced toward the vice president. Her faced burned with embarrassment. "I'm sorry," she said. She unwrapped the ruined newspaper from her foot and held it out to him. The quiet bodyguard took it from her and suddenly burst into uncontrollable laughter. His laugh was more like a giggle. Barbary felt another wave of embarrassment rise across her face. Shreds of newspaper floated around the vice president like a halo, and Frank snatched at them, still scowling. The vice president opened his hands. The last pieces of paper floated away.

"Well, never mind," he said to Barbary. "But do try not to do it again."

"It really is okay," Jeanne said. "Wait till you hear some of the stuff I did before I was used to it."

She swooped to their seats. "Easy, now, right this way. Relax, and just a touch . . ."

Barbary put her feet against the ceiling, held tight to her

23

jacket, and pushed off very, very gently. She moved so slowly she was afraid she would stop before she got across the space between her and Jeanne, but she reached out, being very careful, and Jeanne grasped her fingers.

"Perfect!"

The other passengers applauded. Doubly embarrassed, Barbary ducked down in her seat.

# Chapter Three

The shuttle neared *Outrigger*. If Barbary had not read so much about space, she would never have recognized the space transport as a ship. She had grown up in a world of jets and bullet-trains: sleek, slender, streamlined conveyances. *Outrigger* looked like a cross between a Tinkertoy and a spider web. Struts and towers, antennas and solar panels poked out at every angle.

The transport ship filled the screen with its awkward form, expanding as the shuttle approached. Soon the exterior camera showed only a featureless metal panel. Barbary wished again for windows.

With an almost imperceptible vibration, the shuttle docked against *Outrigger*. The doors of the shuttle's cargo bay nestled into the transport.

"Good work!" Jeanne whispered. She glanced at Barbary and smiled. "Sometimes these dockings shake your teeth. Nice to know we've had a good pilot."

"Can't you find out beforehand?"

25

"Sure," Jeanne said. "But that would spoil all the fun."
She sighed. "I used to know all the shuttle pilots, but so
many joined while I was away . . ."

The shuttle bay doors folded open. People from the
transport floated into the passenger compartment and began
helping the newcomers out of their harnesses.

"It takes half an hour to unload everybody one by one,"
Jeanne said. "Are you game to go with me?"

"Sure," Barbary said.

One of the transport crew propelled himself Jeanne's way.

"Hi, Dr. Velory," he said. "I didn't realize you were
coming in on this flight."

"I thought I'd better," she said, unfastening her harness
and floating beside him. "All things considered." She unfastened Barbary's seat belt.

"Yes," he said. "I expect you're right."

"I'll see that Barbary gets where she's going," Jeanne said.
She indicated Barbary with a flick of her eyes, not a nod of
her head.

"Thanks," the crew member said in a low voice. "Almost
everybody else this trip is a first-timer. Keeping them sorted
out is going to be . . . oh . . . lots of fun."

Barbary found herself hovering out of reach of anything,
drifting toward the transport. Jeanne barely touched her.
She stopped moving.

"For now, I'll just tow you, okay?" She slid Barbary's
duffel bag from beneath the seat. Barbary snatched it. Jeanne
kept her from tumbling away, but glanced at her with a
quizzical expression. Embarrassed to have been so rude,

Barbary dropped her gaze. But she had things with her that she did not want anyone to suspect.

"Grab my belt," Jeanne said.

Barbary slipped her arm through the strap of the duffel bag so she could hang on to Jeanne. She felt awkward and uneasy. But Jeanne pushed off with both feet and sailed straight out of the shuttle.

The shuttle bay doors opened into a large chamber. Supporting struts, handholds, bright-painted lines, and narrow plastic tracks patterned the walls. Everything was a "wall," for nothing was "up" or "down," "floor" or "ceiling."

"I read a lot of novels about space travel," Barbary said. "In them everybody gets around by sticking themselves to the walls with Velcro."

"That doesn't work very well," Jeanne said. "Hook pollution." In response to Barbary's questioning glance, she said, "The little plastic hooks on the Velcro break off and float around and get into things. You can slide along the tracks if you get some skates, or a skating-chair," Jeanne said over her shoulder. "But this way's a lot faster." Jumping, ricocheting, handswimming, she drew Barbary into a maze of corridors and tunnels. In a few minutes Barbary felt completely disoriented. The painted lines joined their course or peeled off from it, disappearing down other corridors. Soon all the colors had changed but one.

"Are you following the blue?"

Jeanne pulled herself along hand over hand. She slowed, glancing at the wall below — beside? — them. "Right," she said. "It *is* blue to deck one. After a while you learn your way around, and you forget which colors lead where."

She accelerated again. She moved in a way almost like crawling, except that she did not use her legs. She kept her body parallel to the surface containing whichever holds she happened to be using at the time. Jeanne grabbed a rung, pulled to propel herself forward, and used her other hand to catch another rung several body-lengths along the corridor.

"Deck one," Barbary said. "What's that?"

"The observation bubble," Jeanne said. "It's quite a sight."

Barbary had dreamed about her first view of space. She had had the dream much longer than she had known she would ever get to see it for real. She barely even remembered a time before she would occasionally wake contented from that fantasy. But one thing was more important to her.

"If we hurry," Jeanne said, "we can watch the shuttle undocking. Then I'll have to get to work. But the sight's worth some extra time."

"Jeanne . . ." Barbary said hesitantly.

"Yeah?"

"I'd like to see that, but I want to . . . I need . . . I'm awfully tired. If I could just go to my room and be alone for a while . . ."

"There's a bathroom near the observation deck, if that's what you need," Jeanne said with an understanding grin. "Do you know how to use a zero-gravity toilet?"

"They give you an instruction booklet when you buy your ticket," Barbary said, a bit embarrassed. "It isn't that. I want to see what you want to show me. But I have to be by myself for a while." She could not explain any further.

"Okay," Jeanne said, sounding puzzled.

Jeanne hovered in the doorway of Barbary's room. "You're sure you're all right."

"Yes," Barbary said. "Thanks."

Jeanne waited another moment, as if to let Barbary change her mind, as if to give her one more chance to trust her. Barbary remained silent. She could feel the secret pocket. She had to be alone immediately.

"I may not see you during the trip, ' Jeanne said. "I'm afraid I'm going to be pretty busy from here on out. But good luck."

"Thanks," Barbary said.

Jeanne pulled the door shut.

Afraid she had failed a test, the first one, a very important one, Barbary wondered if Jeanne thought her a coward, or, perhaps worse, uninterested in her new home.

She had the feeling that she had thrown away Jeanne's proffered friendship, and that Jeanne seldom had time to give anyone a second chance.

She put the fears out of her mind. She had an important task.

She took off her jacket, and found herself spinning free.

Gently, she reminded herself. Move gently.

Clutching her jacket, she kicked toward the wall and grabbed the netting that would form her bed. One-handed, she inched across the tiny room till she reached its small folding table. Nearby hung a couple of loops. She stuck her feet in them. Feeling more solid, she pulled the table out

29

flat. It had straps and a net and a couple of snaps. She laid her jacket inside-out on the table, jury-rigged a harness over it, and unfastened the top of the secret pocket.

She reached inside. Her heart beat fast. She thought she had felt motion, but now she was not sure. Her fingers brushed a silky softness, textured in tabby stripes.

She drew Mickey from the secret pocket. She felt his warmth through his smooth fur. She lifted him and held him to her, pressing her ear against his side, but she could hear only her own pounding heart.

Mickey batted his soft paw against her cheek as he reached out sleepily for a curl of her hair. She lowered him long enough to see him blink his yellow eyes and bristle his long white whiskers in a slow cat yawn.

She buried her face against the tabby cat's side and burst into tears of relief.

Heading toward the research station, *Outrigger* accelerated. The slow increase in velocity left the passengers with a vague feeling of where "down" was, but so little weight that they might as well have been in zero g. Barbary hovered in her cabin, holding Mickey in her arms. Except for the table, the furniture in the cabin consisted of D-rings, straps, and nets fastened to the wall. Nobody sat in chairs in zero g, because chairs were uncomfortable. Without gravity or a harness to draw one's body against the shape of the chair, a person had to consciously hold their body in the right position. It was tiring and eventually painful, especially to the stomach muscles. Barbary found it easy — and much more comfortable than the softest chair — to float, completely relaxed. She drifted in the direction of "down." She could either hover along the floor, barely touching it, like a fish resting on the bottom of the ocean, or she could push off into the air. If she wanted to nap and not move around too much, she could tether herself to the wall.

She stroked Mickey's side. He lay quiet. He would be awake soon, but he would be groggy for at least a couple of hours. She knew that by now, for she had watched him awaken from the sleeping drug twice before, the two times she had carried him back from the spaceport after she had been bumped off her reserved seat.

She had only expected to have to make him go to sleep once or twice. She was worried about the effects of all the sedatives on the small cat.

If they'd let us on board the first time, Barbary thought, this would all be over. We'd already be on the research station. I wouldn't have had to drug him so often. And I wouldn't have had to run away that last time to get another pill.

She shifted her position angrily and abruptly. The reaction sent her tumbling across the room. She rebounded from the wall. She held Mick close with one arm and flailed around with the other, but nothing was in reach. She was annoyed, but she made herself relax and wait till she had drifted to the floor. She stood. Even that took caution. A step was as good as a leap. She pushed off with one toe and floated.

"We're in space, Mick," she said. She stroked him. "It's pretty weird at first, but you get used to it. It's kind of fun.

Are you all right?" She wondered how he would react to zero g. She hoped it would not scare him.

She stroked him again. It was a good feeling. His cinnamon-colored stripes had a different texture from his black fur. He had white paw tips and a white chest. He was only half-grown — he had been a kitten when she found him. If Barbary had been forced to wait for next month's transport, Mickey would have grown too big to hide in the secret pocket. She had no idea what she would have done then.

She smoothed his whiskers and scratched him under the chin, his favorite spot. He licked her hand, two quick warm scratchy touches, and she laughed with relief. He was going to be all right.


Mickey adapted much faster than Barbary to the almost nonexistent gravity. Acceleration, she reminded herself, not really gravity. But, after all, Albert Einstein himself showed that the two were indistinguishable.

Perhaps Mick did so well because, being a cat, he knew he was a superior sort of creature. The first time he tried to run, he left the floor at the first stride like a cartoon cat, running along in place with his feet touching nothing. The second time, he jumped and sailed. He found it unsurprising that he could suddenly, without warning, fly.

Barbary had one piece of sleeping pill left for him. She would have to use it in three days to make him lie quiet when she took him from *Outrigger* to the research station. She had some food for him. She even had some cat litter, but it would spill all over if he dug in it in such low gravity.

Back on earth, when they lived in an apartment, Mick had learned to use the same toilet people used. A lot of cats learned how to do that. The toilet in the tiny bathroom was a weird vacuum arrangement, but Barbary thought Mick would understand that it was the same thing, and that he would use it if the vacuum did not frighten him too much. Luckily, not very many things frightened Mick.

Otherwise I might have to get diapers for him, she thought, and could not help giggling. But the problem was too serious to keep her laughing for long.

If he kept quiet and no one barged into Barbary's room, she might get away with smuggling him onto the science station. But if the room started smelling bad, someone would notice. Then they would be sunk.

Mickey bounced from the floor to the table, landing softly and holding himself there by hooking his claws into the net. He gave one paw a couple of licks, blinked, and drew his legs against his body. That left him drifting just above the table, as if he had suddenly learned how to levitate. He closed his eyes. Usually he curled up to sleep, with one paw over his nose. If he had had a tail he would have wrapped it around his front paws, but he was a Manx cat so he had no tail.

Barbary wondered if curling up in zero g was as hard for a cat as sitting in a chair was for a human being.

She stroked Mick, and he started to purr.

"That's right," she said. "You take it easy. You have a nap and be very quiet and I'll go try to find us something to eat."

She waited until the purring stopped. Normally he slept

33

lightly. Barbary hoped he would only wake for a moment when she left and then go back to sleep, not get curious and try to follow her.

Cracking open the door, Barbary peered into the empty, color-striped corridor. She slipped out. The door had neither a lock nor a Do Not Disturb sign. There was no help for that. She would arouse suspicions if she spent the whole trip in her room. The authorities might decide she was spacesick and therefore unable to live on the research station. Then they would send her back to earth. If she acted normal and stayed out of the way, probably no one would even notice her.

She had to find a dining hall. The cat food hidden in her baggage would only last a little while. She wanted to save it for emergencies.

And, if she was honest with herself, she was dying to see the rest of the ship, particularly Jeanne's observation deck.


In the corridors of the ship, most of the colored stripes lay on the surface that was "down," and the ringlike handholds hung from the surface that had become the ceiling. The gravity was so feeble that Barbary knew she could jump, catch the rings, and swing herself along as if she were on monkey-bars. She decided that first she had better get more experience moving around.

She had to pay close attention to where she was going so she would not get lost. She followed the blue line, but every time she passed a corridor another blue line came out and joined the one she was following. The lines flowed together

34

like small streams meeting larger rivers. She used the angle of their joining to decide which way to go, but she had no way to be sure that was what she was supposed to do.

People had to be able to reach the observation deck from all parts of the ship, so no unique line led there from her cabin. Some color would lead back to her section, but she had not yet been able to figure out which one it was. Again she wished she had a map.

The corridors became more complicated, and though several other blue direction-markers had joined hers, the corridor narrowed rather than widened. The floor became a maze of multicolored lines. In the artificial light of the passageway, the darker colors looked alike.

The blue line followed a ladder upward through a hatchway. Barbary climbed the rungs. At the last one, the line ended.

She looked up, and gasped.

No photograph, no space films, had anything to do with what surrounded her now. She climbed through the hatch to a wide, semicircular platform and stood staring out into the night. The sun was behind them, so the viewing platform was in shadow lit only by stars. But the stars were fantastic. Barbary thought she must be able to see a hundred times as many as on earth, even in the country where sky-glow and smog did not hide them. They spanned the universe, all colors, shining with a steady, cold, remote light. She wanted to write down what they looked like, but every phrase she could think of sounded silly and inadequate.

More than the liftoff, more than weightlessness, the stars let her believe she was really here.

\* \*

Barbary stayed on the viewing platform much longer than she meant to, much longer than she should have. Only her anxiety about Mickey drove her from it. She climbed down the ladder in a sort of daze. From now on, if she were not sent home, if everything worked out, she would never be very far from these calm, clear stars.

The pale gray walls of the ship, solid and dull, brought her back to what she needed to do. She retraced the blue line to the spot where another major line, one in green, split off from the skein. She followed it. She had not seen or heard another person since leaving her room.

The VIPs probably have a fancier part of the ship, she thought, to keep herself from feeling how spooky it was to be alone.

The green line led not to a cafeteria but to something even better, a foyer displaying a map of the ship.

Barbary searched out the colors that led to the places she needed. The 24-hour ship's clock above the map also helped her get her bearings. The clock read 0300: three o'clock in the morning. She was not certain what time zone of earth *Outrigger* and *Einstein* used to set their clocks, but she supposed most everybody must be trying to adjust to the transport's schedule. That would explain why the ship seemed deserted. Everyone else was sleeping. She was just as glad. This way there was less chance of Mickey's being discovered while she was gone.

Anxious again, Barbary started along the line that led to the cafeteria. She wondered why they had chosen purple.

Forgetting to slide along as if she were skating, she took one running step. The next thing she knew she bounced off the ceiling. Unhurt but dizzy, she ricocheted and tumbled from ceiling to floor to ceiling before she managed to grab a handhold. She let herself drift to the floor. She tried to copy the smooth skating motion she had seen on tapes of people in space. The trick was to propel herself forward without shoving herself up at the same time. She still felt awkward, but she was getting where she was going.

An open door led into the deserted cafeteria. Barbary dug around in her pockets for coins to work the automated servers, then realized none was necessary. Meals came with one's passage, she supposed. And it must not be too often that a stowaway ate food never paid for.

She chose a couple of chicken sandwiches, plus two balloon-like containers of milk. She wished she had a bag, or that she had worn her jacket, so she could hide things in its pockets. Next time she would remember. She stuck the sandwiches under her shirt and held the bulbs of milk in one hand, leaving her other hand free.

Halfway to her room, when she began to think she would have the luck not to meet anyone, she heard voices. She spun, intending to hide in a branch corridor. But she had pushed off with too much force. She left the floor as if she had jumped, hit the ceiling, and rebounded, spinning helplessly toward the deck.

Jeanne Velory and a member of the ship's crew glided around the bend in the hall. Concentrating on a thick sheaf of print-outs, they did not notice her tumbling toward them.

"Look out!" Barbary cried. They spun out of her vision.

Jeanne caught her, bringing Barbary to a halt while Jeanne herself barely moved. She pulled Barbary to a handhold. Barbary grabbed it, her face burning with embarrassment. She still clutched the bulbs of milk.

"A new recruit, huh?" the crew member said, a hint of amusement in her tone. Anger would have been easier for Barbary to take.

"We all choose our own mealtimes here," Jeanne said to Barbary, her voice neutral. "The cafeteria's always open, so you don't have to take food to your room between times. It isn't a good idea — the recycling system isn't set up for that. I'm sorry no one explained it to you."

"Oh," Barbary said.

"Are you hurt?"

"No."

"Can you find your way back?"

"Yeah."

"Okay. Come on, Valya."

Barbary watched them go, then angrily scrubbed her sleeve across her eyes.

If she doesn't want to be friends, Barbary thought, just because I can't do exactly what she wants me to, exactly when she wants me to do it, then, tough. That's an adult for you.

Slowly, this time, Barbary headed for her room.

# Chapter Four

Her pulse raced. Barbary stopped. Afraid she would find an irritated crew member holding Mickey by the scruff of his neck, she peeked around the corner.

Her door remained shut, the hallway silent. Barbary crept to her room, opened the door, and slipped inside.

"Mick?" Mickey was nowhere to be seen. "Hey, Mick?" she said again, worried.

Mickey bounded from behind her rumpled jacket and landed against her. He curled in the crook of her arm, purring.

"Hi," she said, relieved. "I'm glad you kept out of trouble." She grinned ruefully. "You're doing better than me."

She opened one of the bulbs, extended its straw, and squeezed out a glob of milk. Mickey sniffed it. It bounced back and forth, in and out. The sphere flattened, then stretched into a long sausage shape. Never having seen milk behave so strangely, Mick bristled his whiskers and drew away.

"Don't get picky," Barbary said. "It wasn't exactly easy getting this for you."

She coaxed him till he lapped at the quivering white blob. Mickey drank milk even more messily in space than he did back on earth. Droplets flew from the tip of the bulb, beading into spheres before bursting onto Barbary's shirt or drifting like soap bubbles to the floor. She offered him some chicken, but after sniffing it, he ignored it. She tried to get him to eat a bit of the dry food from her duffel bag, but he showed no more interest in that. He snuggled against her shoulder, closed his eyes, and fell asleep.

Barbary put Mickey on her jacket and cleaned up the spilled milk. She ate a chicken sandwich and drank the other bulb of milk. Then, yawning, she had to figure out how to arrange the sleeping net. Instructions posted beside it claimed to show the way it worked, but it turned out to be much more complicated. When she finally fixed it so she thought she could get into it, she felt exhausted. Though her room was warm enough, she wished she had a blanket to wrap herself in. She remembered a little kid much younger than she, in the group home on earth. He had been inseparable from his old tattered blanket. Right now Barbary understood how he had felt; she wished she had never made fun of him.

She climbed awkwardly into the net, fastened it, and fell fast asleep. When Mickey crawled in beside her, she halfway woke, then went immediately back to sleep.


By sleeping during the ship's daytime and only going out of her room when nearly everybody else was in bed, Barbary made it through the three days of the journey from low earth orbit to the research station without Mickey's being discovered. Under normal circumstances, somebody would probably have noticed her weird behavior. But with all the VIPs to take care of and everybody curious and worried and wondering about the approaching alien ship, no one cared what Barbary did. She smuggled food to Mickey in the secret pocket of her jacket, then sneaked the wrappers and milk bulbs back to the recycling bins. Maybe it was a good thing that Jeanne Velory had reproved her, for without the warning, she might have clogged up the waste chute in her room. If someone came to fix it they would have discovered Mickey.

The problem she had worried most about, after keeping Mick hidden, turned out to be not much of a problem at all. The first time Mick heard the vacuum pump attached to the toilet, he bristled his fur and hissed, but after he realized it was not a big creature that would jump out and get him, he ignored the pump and used the facilities as if they were just like the ones back on earth.

When she could, Barbary explored the ship. She spent a lot of time in the observation bubble. She wanted to take Mickey there and show it to him, but she kept changing her mind about how risky that would be. She never saw anyone else inside the bubble. Maybe VIPs went into space so often that they did not care. Barbary found it impossible to imagine getting tired of the sight.

She did sometimes see people in the cafeteria, even in the middle of the night. Usually they were talking about the alien ship, speculating and supposing. Barbary listened to them, but soon realized that Jeanne had told her everything anyone knew for certain. They would have to wait till they reached *Einstein*, and the alien ship near it, to find out anything more.

One of the research station's missions was to search for gravity waves. For that it had to be well away from earth and the moon. That was the reason for its long polar orbit. It reached its greatest distance from earth, its apogee, above the northern hemisphere. Since the alien ship approached on a path well above the plane of the solar system, *Einstein* was the best place from which to observe the ship's passing. Or to contact it, if, as Jeanne believed, it carried living beings.

But as the alien ship drifted farther and farther into the solar system, it showed no sign of life. It continued to ignore radio signals. Many people argued that the ship must be under conscious control, for the chances of its passing so close to the solar system were otherwise terribly small. But others continued to think that the ship must have been drifting, dead, for millions for years. They thought it was only luck that brought the ship near enough to notice.


The days passed. *Einstein* appeared first as a large bright spot, then as a sparkly Christmas tree ornament, finally as a huge spinning double wheel growing larger each minute. A few hours before docking, *Outrigger's* acceleration stopped. The transport had reached a velocity just slightly greater than the velocity of *Einstein*; soon it would catch up to the station. *Outrigger's* steering rockets vibrated softly, orienting the transport to dock.

42

Barbary knew she had to go to the debarkation lounge and strap in with the other passengers. But as long as she could, she delayed leaving her room. Feeling nervous, she checked for the hundredth time to be sure she had left nothing behind. She had hardly anything to forget. Her bag had been packed for hours.

"All passengers proceed to debarkation lounge immediately. Fifteen minutes to docking burn."

The intercom had begun broadcasting the message an hour before. The "immediately" was new. Pretty soon somebody would probably come to fetch stragglers. But Barbary procrastinated, so she could put off drugging Mick till the last minute. She did not know how long it would be before she could find a private place where it would be safe for him to wake.

Barbary unbuttoned her pants pocket and took out a small white envelope. It contained a broken chunk of pill, the last bit of sedative. She wondered, as she always did, if it was the right size. She had had to break up a tranquilizer meant for a person, and estimate how much to give Mickey. That was one of the reasons she was afraid the drug might kill him. Mick watched her, unblinking, as she pushed toward him with the pill hidden in her hand.

"You know I've got it, don't you?" she said. "I know you don't like it, but you have to take it. Unless you want to lie still in my pocket for the next couple of hours. Fat chance."

She reached for him. He stretched his body till his hind feet touched a wall, leaped, and sailed past her.

"Mickey!" she said, louder than she meant to. "Come on, don't play, we can't afford it."

43

He touched the far wall with his front paws and bounded, turning a back flip. He maneuvered with certainty and grace even in weightlessness, while Barbary still felt awkward.

"If you had a tail, I could understand," she said. "You'd use it to balance with."

Mick sailed from wall to wall to wall like a bird, or at least a flying squirrel. He spread himself out like a squirrel when he leaped, and the stub where his tail would have been twitched back and forth.

Barbary stopped trying to catch him. She waited till he got tired of springing faster and faster back and forth. He caught his claws in a net to stop himself. Maybe he had made himself dizzy, because when he retracted his claws, he floated away from the wall without kicking off.

He watched her upside down.

He was vulnerable while he was floating. Barbary caught him in midair.

"Ha," she said. "Outsmarted yourself, didn't you?"

Barbary held Mick against her body so she could feed him the pill. She had to steady him with her left arm, open his mouth with her left hand, and stick the pill down his throat with her right hand. He growled as she forced his jaws apart. Since she had no free hand with which to steady herself, she tumbled in a slow circle.

"Shh," she said to Mick. "It isn't that bad."

He bit her and she yelped, but she kept hold of him and pushed the pill to the back of his tongue as he tried to twist away from her. She held his mouth shut and stroked his throat to help him swallow.

"There, see? Now you'll go to sleep and when you wake

up — ouch!" He dug in his claws and jumped. She let him elude her. He hovered in the farthest corner, growling, his fur fluffed up. Barbary waited. After five minutes his growling faltered as he began to feel drowsy. His eyelids drooped, and he meowed. Barbary floated to him and took him in her arms.

"I'm sorry, Mick, I know you hate it. I don't know what's going to happen, either. I hope everything will be all right when you wake up. For a change." She cuddled him till he went limp with sleep.

Barbary slid him into the secret pocket, put on the baggy jacket, grabbed her duffel bag, and hurried out just as the intercom clicked on again. "All passengers to the disembarkation deck. Urgent. All passengers —"


Barbary trembled with nervousness. She had arrived at the lounge in plenty of time to strap in before the burn. Nevertheless, one of the crew members had hustled her to a seat and bawled her out. Now it seemed as though she had been sitting there for hours, because of course the docking burn was not fifteen minutes away, but nearer forty-five. Barbary tried to concentrate on the sight of *Einstein*, a vast wheel within a wheel spinning in the center of a TV screen as *Outrigger* approached its hub. But her attention kept returning to Mickey's warm weight in the secret pocket.

Jeanne Velory was the last person to get to the lounge. Barbary hoped she would see her and smile at her, or even just nod, but she did not. She strapped herself in, leaned back, and closed her eyes. For a moment, strain showed in

45

her face. It had never before occurred to Barbary that Jeanne might be nervous about her new job, her new home, and the alien ship on top of everything else. How could she *not* be nervous?

Barbary still envied her, but she felt a little sorry for her, too, and she wished she had been able to be more honest with her.

What difference does it make? Barbary thought. She's too important. She'd never have time to be friends anyway.

*Outrigger* suddenly vibrated. *Einstein* appeared to move slightly as the transport's orientation changed. The steering rockets guided them. Barbary grew almost sure she could feel another motion, that of Mickey waking up. The sedative should have kept him asleep much longer. Barbary wondered if he could have developed a resistance to the sleeping drug . . . A moment later she felt just as sure that he lay too still, that he had stopped breathing. Maybe this time the sedative had been too much for him.

She prevented herself from reaching inside the secret pocket.

The *clang*, transmitted through the skin of the transport as it docked against *Einstein*, scared her for a moment. She caught her breath.

They had reached the research station.

She was home.

Maybe she would get to stay here. But she had thought she had found home, other times, and she had always been sent away.

Without Jeanne to vouch for her, Barbary had to wait to be unstrapped and taken into the station. At the very last, when everybody else had disembarked, a crew member freed her and towed her out of the lounge. Barbary felt embarrassed that he assumed she was completely incompetent in zero g.

Inside the research station, the crew member maneuvered Barbary over and through the chaos of the waiting room. People floated free, dangled from handholds, or let crew members strap them into the skating-chairs that moved along the narrow tracks in the walls. The crew member deposited her at a web strap.

"You're being met?"

Barbary nodded.

"Okay. Stay here till they find you."

After the crew member left, Barbary realized she did not even know for sure if anyone knew she was on this flight. She should have tried to call them from *Outrigger*, but she had been so concerned about keeping out of sight and keeping Mick hidden that she never thought to try. It was too late now.

She hooked one arm through the web strap and held on to her duffel bag with the same hand, then took the chance of reaching into the secret pocket. Her fingers brushed Mickey's soft fur. He was lying very, very still.

"Let me carry that, okay?"

Barbary felt a tug on her duffel bag. She snatched it back and jerked her hand away from Mick.

"I'll carry it myself!" She flopped around like a hooked fish and finally came to rest facing the person who had spoken to her.

She did not recognize her at first. Barbary knew that

47

Heather was her own age, but the little girl hovering before her was much smaller, very thin, and looked only eight or nine. She had hardly any color to her skin, though her hair and eyes were black. Who else could she be *but* Heather?

"Jeez," she said, "what's the matter?"

Barbary was too embarrassed to admit she had reacted as she would have back on earth. Nobody would try to steal anything out here. For one thing — where would they go?

"You surprised me," Barbary said. "I just like to carry my own stuff, okay?"

"Sure. You *are* Barbary, aren't you? Dumb question, you have to be. I'm Heather. We're practically sisters." Heather sounded far less fragile than she looked.

Maybe people who are born on space stations are just naturally littler, Barbary thought.

"Hi," she said. She had meant to begin well here. She hoped she had not already started to make a mess of everything.

"Aren't you hot in that jacket? You don't need it here on Atlantis." Heather wore shorts and a tank top.

"Atlantis?" Barbary tried to divert the conversation so Heather would not get suspicious about her jacket. And, besides — *Atlantis?*

Heather grinned. "That isn't the official name, I know, but that's what we all call it. Atlantis was a mythical continent. Its people were supposed to have a high-tech civilization when all the other human beings were still wrapping themselves up in animal skins."

"Yeah," Barbary said, "but Atlantis sank."

"That's a good point," Heather said. "I hadn't thought of

that. I guess nobody else did, either. Do you know how to sly yet?"

"Huh?"

"Sly. That's 'swim' and 'fly' — it's how you get around in zero g."

"A little, I guess," Barbary said. "But I can't do it very well."

"Okay, I'll tow you. It's a lot faster than getting you a chair, and they're pretty silly anyway. People only use them who are too chicken to try slying." Heather took Barbary's hand. "Come on, let's go find Yoshi. He's looking for you, too."

Barbary untangled herself and her duffel bag from the web strap. Heather pushed off. Barbary relaxed and let herself be towed. She kept a tight hold on her bag. If it got loose and banged against something, it might come untied. It would be ridiculous if she smuggled Mickey on board but got caught because the cat food spilled all over. Afraid of the drug's effect on Mick, she both hoped and feared to feel him move. She *would not* look toward him. If she pretended nothing was unusual, nothing was wrong, she would not see a white-tipped tabby paw push through the front of her coat, opening the way for a pink nose and white whiskers . . .

Heather got all the way to the other side of the doughnut-shaped room without running into a single dignitary. Considering the crowd and the confusion, that was quite a feat.

"There's Yoshi!" Heather said. "Yoshi! I found her!"

Yoshi rotated as Heather swooped toward him. He caught them both and swung them around and to a stop. Heather

49

laughed. Barbary swallowed hard and clutched the duffel bag.

"Where's Thea?" Heather asked.

"I don't know," Yoshi said. "She said she'd come, but I guess she forgot."

Yoshi, Heather's father and Barbary's mother's best friend from college, was of medium height, compact and athletic. Barbary liked his smile. He had none of Heather's frailty, but she had his good looks and dark hair and eyes.

Yoshi gave Barbary a hug. "Barbary, I'm very glad you're here." He held her away to look at her, and hugged her again. In the air above them, Heather did free somersaults, turning fast twice, her knees hugged to her chest, then stretching out her arms and legs to spin once slowly. She caught a strap and stopped.

Barbary suddenly felt quite shy. She did not know what to say to Yoshi, nor how to thank him for all he had done, without sounding silly and sentimental.

"I'm glad I'm here, too," she said. "I didn't think they'd ever let me come."

"It should never have taken so long," Yoshi said. "And after all that, to have to fight with every diplomat on earth just for a shuttle ticket —" He shook his head, then smiled again. "You look a lot like your mother."

Barbary shrugged. "I don't know."

"Haven't you even seen a picture of her?"

Barbary shook her head. "Not for a long time. I had some stuff, but it got lost. I don't know. I don't remember." She did remember. She used to have some smoke-damaged photographs, and a ring. In one of the places she stayed, the ring disappeared. In another, they threw away her photos as a punishment. She pretended not to care, because she would not give anyone the satisfaction of hurting her. Who cared about a bunch of old pictures, you couldn't see anything on them anyway. That's what she said out loud.

It was true that the images were out of focus, obscured by time and misfortune, and only two-dimensional anyway. She had no clear memory of her mother's face, either from life or from pictures. But she did care.

"I've got a couple of snapshots," Yoshi said. "They're from a long time ago, but still . . . I'll get you some copies."

Yoshi glanced at the diplomats and assistants and secretaries who surrounded them. Most of them looked awkward and uncomfortable in zero g. "This crowd will be about as useful as a flock of sheep." To Barbary he said, "Did anyone tell you what's happened?"

"Yes," she said. "But it's still a secret back on earth."

"They're afraid an announcement will make the grounders panic," Heather said.

"I didn't panic," Barbary said.

"But you're not a grounder anymore."

"Grounder or not has nothing to do with it," Yoshi said. "More than a handful of people should know what's going on. When we meet that ship — it's history. Even if it's a derelict. That's the majority view. Which I don't subscribe to." He reached for Barbary's hand. "Aren't you hot in that jacket?"

"No. Yes. A little. It's easier to wear it than carry it."

"Okay. Ready?"

Barbary nodded.

Yoshi and Heather pushed off, towing Barbary behind them.

Yoshi sailed from wall to brace to floor, around small groups of people, past doors and monkey-bars and tracks. He oriented himself as if the edge of the doughnut-shaped room were the floor, and the flat top and bottom its edges. Barbary would have put herself ninety degrees the other way, so the flat parts of the room were floor and ceiling, and the curving places were walls. That would have felt more natural. Farther out toward the rim of the station, the curving wall *would* be the floor, so Yoshi's orientation made more sense. Heather, when she was not holding Barbary's hand, paid no attention at all to walls or floor or ceiling. She swooped from one point to another, turned upside-down or sideways to the direction her father was facing. She acted as if she saw no difference at all.

They slyed over the juncture between spinning and non-spinning parts of the station. The slow relative motion was hardly noticeable. They got into one of the elevators. It had a weird paint job: white footprints on the surface of one wall, which was green, and the outlines of people on the beige wall opposite the elevator door.

"This will be the floor when we reach bottom," Yoshi said, indicating the footprints. "But *this* wall will tilt on the way down." He used a strap to hold himself against the wall with the outlines, and to keep his feet on the surface with the footprints. Heather did the same.

"You want to be pretty firmly planted," Yoshi said. "Between the momentum and the spin, it's a fairly strange feeling." He drew Barbary beside him.

The elevator started to move. Barbary felt as if she were leaning against a steeply tilted wall. Startled, she grabbed Yoshi and held on, afraid they were going to crash.

"It's okay," Yoshi said. "You see what I mean."

"It's *supposed* to work like this?"

"This is the way the laws of physics make it work."

As they fell, the tilt changed, making Barbary feel as if she were standing more and more upright.

Heather seemed not even to notice the odd sensation. "Turn around," she said, "and look over this way."

"What?" Barbary suspected a trick, for Heather was directing her to face the side wall. "Why?"

"Just do it, trust me, quick!" She pushed Barbary around, not very hard. Barbary could have resisted, but she decided to give Heather a chance. She faced the wall. It was glass — she had not realized that till now because the metal casing beyond was featureless and very smooth.

Its edge passed up the window, like a shade rising, and suddenly Barbary was looking out at the station, from inside it, with the universe beyond.

"Ohh . . ." she said. Heather squeezed her hand.

The stars were as beautiful as they had been from the observation deck of the transport ship. But the overwhelming sight was the station, a huge wheel within a wheel spinning past the stars. As they dropped through one of the spokes, the wheels grew larger, much larger than she had expected, even knowing the dimensions, even seeing the station on the screen in the transport's lounge.

Shadows in space were very black and distinct. Some distance away, a silvery craft sprang suddenly into view. Invis-

53

ible one moment, the next it was in plain sight. Nothing was out there for it to hide behind — then Barbary understood that it had been in the shadow of the station. She was used to thinking of shadows as falling on a surface, not as great lightless volumes of space stretching out into infinity. She shivered.

"It's beautiful," she said to Heather.

"I want to show you everything! We can drop off your bag and go see the labs and the garden and the observatory —"

"You mean right now?" Barbary said, stricken.

"Sure!"

"Heather, honey, Barbary's been traveling for a long time, she's tired," Yoshi said. "Let's get her settled before you two start exploring."

"Okay, sure, that makes sense," Heather said, sounding downcast. "But there's an awful lot to see, and you need to be able to find your way around."

"Hold tight," Yoshi said. "Feet on the floor?"

The elevator braked. Barbary's stomach lurched. She was afraid that after all, after going through everything, now at the end of the trip she would throw up. She fought down the queasiness.

The tilt vanished: the floor steadied and leveled out. They had stopped at the inner wheel, which was about halfway to the outside rim of the station. Barbary thought she weighed maybe half here what she did on earth. It was hard to tell, though, after several days in nearly zero g. The elevator doors opened. Yoshi and Heather glided out.

"Why did we stop on this level?" Barbary asked.

54

"We live on this level," Yoshi said.

"Oh . . . The booklet said all the living quarters are out on the rim." The rim rotated with an acceleration of one gravity.

"Most of them are," Yoshi said. "But we live here."

Heather, walking faster, left Yoshi and Barbary a little way behind. Barbary wondered what it was that she and her father were not telling.

# Chapter Five

Barbary followed Heather. The corridor rose before and behind them, for it followed the arc of the station's inner wheel. But though Barbary could see that the hall curved upward, she felt as if she were walking down a gentle incline. It was a very strange sensation.

Heather turned right, into a crossways hall, and both the curve of the floor and the perception of going down disappeared.

Barbary followed Heather around a second right turn. Now they were walking the opposite direction from the way they had started. Again the hall looked like it rose, but this time Barbary felt as if she were walking up a shallow incline.

She had no chance to ask what was going on. A few paces beyond the corner, Heather opened a door and went inside. Yoshi followed.

Barbary entered a small, sparsely furnished living room.

Of course it had no windows. People who lived in space needed more protection from solar radiation and cosmic rays than glass or plastic could give. The station had lots of observation ports, but Barbary would have to learn to be careful how long she gazed through them, and she would have to keep track of the readings on her radiation tag.

Pictures and posters covered the wall. Barbary had always plastered the walls of her room — whenever she had stayed in one place long enough — with star posters, astronomical artwork, and magazine pictures from the *Ares* mission. Here lakes, forests, meadows, and a long mural of mountains covered the walls. In one corner, though, a sequence of small photos traced the development of a comet. Barbary wanted to look at those more closely.

The kitchen area contained little more than one would need for making coffee or heating soup. No room there for leftovers to steal for Mick. On the other hand, if people ate cafeteria-style, she might have an even easier time getting his food.

She could worry about that later. Right now she needed to make sure he was all right.

"Can I see my room?" she asked.

Heather glided past a basket-weave couch. "I'll show it to you!"

Barbary followed, dragging her duffel bag. It was not very heavy in this gravity, but she was awfully tired.

Heather opened a door. Barbary followed her inside.

Heather jumped more than her own height into the air, spinning, and landed neatly on a bunk.

"Isn't it great?" she said. "We redid it when we knew you were coming. I've been sleeping on the top bunk, but if you like it better we can switch."

Barbary sat down abruptly on a spindly-legged chair. Two matching desks stood nearby. The top of one was bare; the other held tapes and a plush animal.

"I thought . . ." she said, "I thought I was going to get my own room."

Heather sat still, trying to conceal her disappointment.

"But it'll be fun to share the room," Heather said. "Like your mom and my mom and Yoshi and the others rented a house together in college."

"Is that what you expect me to do? Copy my mother?" Barbary said angrily.

"No, that isn't what I meant at all," Heather said, embarrassed. "But it really would be fun. We haven't finished fixing it up yet. I was waiting to see how you wanted it to look."

Barbary hooked her heels on the edge of the chair, hugged her knees to her chest, and gazed at her shoes. The weight of the secret pocket pressed against her side.

"I bet you'll like it if you give it a chance," Heather said.

"I need a lot of privacy. I have stuff of my own that I need to do by myself."

After a moment, Heather jumped from the upper bunk. Her feet made a surprisingly loud and solid *thud* when she landed.

"You can have all the privacy you want, then!" She stamped out and slammed the door behind her.

Barbary stared at the closed door.

She'll never be my friend, either, she thought.

But her worry over Mickey crowded out her unhappiness at having had to drive Heather away. She slipped out of her jacket. Mick had not moved. Barbary opened the secret pocket, reached inside, and touched the cat's soft fur. She hesitated, letting her hand rest on his side, feeling for his heartbeat, for a breath, even for a twitch. She pulled him out of the pocket. He lay limp in her hands.

"Mick, it's okay, wake up, please?" She pressed her ear to his side. At first she heard nothing. She sat up and stroked his smooth tabby side, feeling the texture of his stripes, willing him to move. She bent down again and held her breath to listen.

His paw twitched, and he growled in his sleep.

She sat up, laughing with relief. "You dumb cat," she said. "I'm sitting here afraid you're dead, and you're just dreaming."

Someone knocked on the door. With a quick, scared glance around, Barbary scooped up her jacket and Mickey, dragged open the deep bottom drawer of the desk with the empty top, the one she supposed must be hers, and slid Mick into it.

"Barbary?" Yoshi said. "Can I come in?"

Barbary pushed the drawer shut. It squeaked. She flinched, hoping the noise was inaudible outside. She opened the door and tried to join Yoshi in the living room. But her foster father guided her back into the room. He sat on the bunk and patted the blanket beside him.

"Please sit down, Barbary."

Staring at the floor, Barbary obeyed. So her almost sister had told on her the first chance she got . . .

"Heather looked upset when she came out," Yoshi said. "Did you two have a fight?"

Maybe this bawling out won't be as bad as I thought, Barbary said to herself. Maybe I can get it over with before Mick decides he *has* to get out of that drawer.

"Not a fight, exactly."

"Do you want to tell me about it?"

"It wasn't her fault. I just thought I'd have a room all my own. I didn't mean to hurt her feelings."

"I think you must have, though. Rather badly, the way she looked." He folded one leg under him. He was barefoot. "There are quite a few people on the station. We don't have a lot of living area. As much space as we can, we use for research. And right now, with the extra people, it's very crowded. After they go home, I think we can find a room for you. That's the best I can offer just now. Can you be patient for a while?"

Barbary guessed that the only alternative to patience was going back to earth.

"Yeah," she said. She heard a faint scratching from the desk. "Sure." She would have said almost anything to get Yoshi to leave. "I'm really sorry. I'll tell Heather."

"Good." Yoshi got to his feet. "We're very glad to have you with us. But the environment's different. It's difficult. It takes extra effort to get along, sometimes."

"I understand," Barbary said. "I'll do better from now on."

"Okay." Yoshi went to the door, opened it, and glanced back with a grin. "I'll let Heather know you want to talk to her." He closed the door.

Barbary wanted to shout all the worst words she knew. She stopped herself, but not because she cared right now whether anyone thought she was civilized. She was afraid Yoshi would hear her and wonder what she was still so upset about.

But she did not know what to do. Even if she wanted to drug Mickey again — which she did not — she had no more pills. Besides, she could not keep him drugged all the time. She had concentrated so hard on how to smuggle him off earth that she had never thought about what she would do if she succeeded. Now she had to face that problem.

She heard a louder, more insistent scratching from her desk.

The bedroom door opened and Heather came in.

"Hi," she said, watchful restraint in her voice. "Yoshi says you want to talk to me."

"I didn't mean to hurt your feelings. The room's really nice. It'll be fun to share it. I wouldn't have said what I did, only I'm awfully tired. I need to take a nap before I fall over —"

"Mrrow," the desk said, through Barbary's rush of words.

"What was *that?*" Heather said.

"Nothing. What do you mean? I didn't hear anything."

Mick yowled and scratched frantically. If he did not get his way soon, he would howl so loudly that no one in the apartment could possibly miss it.

Heather looked curiously at the desk.

"What have you got in there?" she said.

Mickey growled. Barbary yanked the drawer open to keep him from screeching. He poked his head out, blinked, and sprang out of his hiding place.

"What's that?" Heather said. "Is that a rabbit? How did you get him up here? What's his name?"

Mickey took a couple of cautious steps, gathered his powerful hind legs under him, and leaped to the top bunk. He walked across it, his paws making small padding noises on the puffy comforter.

"A rabbit! Don't you know anything? He's a cat!" Barbary swung around suddenly and grabbed Heather's shoulders, pushing her hard against the wall. Heather caught her breath in astonishment.

"If you tell anybody —" Barbary said, "if you tell on us and they take Mick away, I'll get you for it if it's the last thing I do!"

"Tell on you? Are you kidding? I've always wanted to see a cat. I never have before." She shrugged Barbary's hands from her shoulders. "Let me go. Boy, are you dumb. Do you really think you can hide him here without my help?"

As Barbary watched in surprise, Heather pushed past her and bounced to the upper bunk, where Mickey was sniffing at corners. He sat down and looked at her, blinking his big yellow eyes.

"He's really neat. How did you get him to the station? No wonder you wanted me out of here. But you should have trusted me first thing. Will he let me touch him?"

"I don't know," Barbary said. "I doubt it. He doesn't like strangers much. He might scratch you."

Heather extended one hand toward him. Barbary stood on the lower bunk with her elbows on the upper one.

"It's okay, Mick, she won't hurt you."

"Does he understand you?"

"Sometimes he seems like he does," Barbary said. "Other times he just ignores you. Cats are like that. He doesn't do what you tell him unless he wants to."

Mickey sniffed at Heather's outstretched fingers, bristled his whiskers, and then, to Barbary's surprise, rubbed his head against Heather's hand.

"Oh," Heather said. "I didn't know he'd be so soft."

Barbary showed Heather how to pet Mickey, using long, smooth strokes going the same way his fur grew. He stretched his hind legs and the nub of his tail stood straight up.

"He really doesn't have a tail!" Heather said. "That's why I thought he was a rabbit. Rabbits have long ears and a short tail and cats have short ears and a long tail. That's what I read. Is he half and half?"

"No, there isn't any such thing as half and half. That would be a mess even if you could do it. Cats eat meat and rabbits eat carrots and stuff. He's a Manx cat. They don't have tails."

"Why not?"

"They just don't."

Heather stroked Mickey. Barbary felt a little jealous that he took to her so quickly. Back on earth, when Barbary found Mick behind the apartment building where she was living, she had coaxed him for two days to get him out of his hidey-hole. And at that, he came out only because he was so hungry he could not resist the smell of the fish she stole for him. Even then, even though he was almost too weak to stand up, he had growled at her every time she came near him. It took her three days to make friends with him.

"How did you get him here? Is that why you didn't want me to carry your bag?"

"Sort of. It's got a couple of boxes of cat food in it. But I couldn't hide Mickey there. It had to go through security, and they would have seen him with the x-ray." She got her jacket out of the drawer and showed Heather the secret pocket.

"That's neat," Heather said. "I never would have thought of it."

"I didn't," Barbary admitted. "I read a bunch of books on magic."

"Magic? Like witches and stuff?"

"Stage magic. Tricks. Sleight of hand. Hiding things you don't want anybody to see. You have to get them to look other places." She pulled out her silver dollar, showed it to Heather, passed her left hand across it and made it disappear, then pulled it out of Heather's ear.

"How'd you do that?"

"I'll show you sometime, if you want to learn how to do it. Otherwise I'm supposed to keep it a secret. Anyway, that's sort of how I hid Mick."

She turned the jacket over so the outside pockets showed. "With this, everybody looks at all the pockets and thinks, 'Isn't that cute,' or something, and they don't notice that there's another pocket on the inside, and a big lump where Mickey is."

"I sure didn't," Heather said.

Mickey finished exploring the upper bunk, stuck his nose in the bookcase at the head of it, walked inside, and curled up. It was a tight fit, but he looked happy.

"Maybe we can train him to stay there when somebody comes in," Heather said. "Nobody would ever see him."

"It's hard to train a cat," Barbary said. "They do what they want. But maybe he'll just decide he likes it there. Then we won't have to train him."

Heather flopped down on the bunk, nose to nose with Mickey. He stretched forward and sniffed her face.

Heather giggled. "His nose is cold!"

"It's supposed to be. If it isn't, that means he's sick."

"Huh. I didn't know that."

"Don't you have any animals up here at all?"

"In the labs, mice and rats and some monkeys. But they have to stay in their cages, because everybody's afraid they'll get away and infest the station. The mice and rats, I mean, not the monkeys."

Barbary started to say that she thought it would be very boring to live somewhere where there were no other animals than people, but then she realized that before she found Mickey, she had never lived around animals, either, and had never particularly missed them. People did not keep pets in cities very much anymore, or if they did they kept them inside all the time. Barbary had never seen a horse or a cow except in a zoo.

"We'll have to be careful," Heather said. "There's a rule against pets on the station. People have been trying to change it for a while, but it's just one of those dumb bureaucratic rules where you *might* get in trouble if you change it, but nothing happens if you don't change it, so you leave it the way it is."

"What will happen if somebody finds him?"

Heather turned over so she could see her.

"Um . . . I don't know."

"You'd get in trouble."

Heather shrugged. "Probably."

"I'd get in trouble."

"Well, yeah."

"What about Mick?"

Heather did not answer for a moment. Then she said, "They'd probably take him away."

At that moment there was a knock on the door.

# Chapter Six

Heather sat up so fast she banged her head against the ceiling. Barbary vaulted to her side.

"Heather? Barbary?" Yoshi said. "If Barbary's going to get a nap before we go to dinner, she'll have to do it now. The reception for Jeanne Velory is at nineteen hundred."

"Ouch," Heather said.

"What did you say?"

"She said okay," Barbary said. She leaned toward Heather. "*Are* you okay?" she whispered.

"Is something wrong?" Yoshi sounded worried, as if he feared Barbary and Heather had really begun to fight. After what had happened earlier, Barbary could not blame him.

The door slid open. Barbary threw herself around to sit against Heather's bookshelf, hiding Mickey.

Yoshi stuck his head into the room. Heather managed to smile, but she had a glazed expression.

"Heather, it wouldn't hurt for you to take a nap, too."

Mickey butted his head against Barbary's back, trying to nudge past her. He pushed his paw between her and the wall, extending his claws to scratch at her side. Barbary was very ticklish. She tried not to squirm.

"Right," Heather said groggily to Yoshi.

"We've just been talking," Barbary said.

"Maybe one of you should sleep in the other room."

"We'll turn out the light and be quiet, honest." Mick's claws dug into the sensitive place under her arm. She caught her breath.

"All right," Yoshi said, though he still looked concerned. "But don't talk the whole time. Agreed?"

"Sure." Barbary's voice sounded funny to her, because she was trying to talk without inhaling or exhaling. As soon as she took a breath, she would begin to giggle.

Yoshi slid the door closed behind him. Heather immediately clapped her hands to her head, and Barbary flung herself forward with a muffled shriek of laughter.

"I'm glad you think it's so funny," Heather whispered.

"I'm sorry," Barbary said. "I wasn't laughing at you. Mick was tickling me. I almost couldn't stand it."

"Okay. But keep quiet or Yoshi'll hear us."

Mickey sauntered out of his hiding place, looked at them both in disdain, and jumped off the bunk.

"Are you okay?" Barbary asked.

"I think so, yeah. I might have a bump. Boy, was that dumb. Running yourself into a ceiling is real kid stuff."

Barbary climbed down from the bunk, picked Mickey up, and cradled him in her arms. "That was close, Mick," she said.

68

Heather jumped down beside her. "We better at least pretend to sleep," she said.

"Yeah, okay."

Heather gestured toward the top bunk. "You better take that one. It'll be safer."

"Are you sure that's okay with you?"

"Uh-huh," Heather said. "But be careful not to sit up too fast."

"Right." Barbary nodded.

The floor twisted beneath her. She staggered, flung one hand out to catch herself, and clutched Mick to her with the other arm. He hissed in protest and tried to jump free.

"Barbary! What's wrong?"

Barbary kept hold of the edge of the bunk, but let Mick loose.

"You mean . . . you didn't feel anything?"

"No," Heather said. "Feel what?"

"The floor . . ." She stopped. Maybe she had something wrong with her, and if anyone found out —

Heather laughed. "I know!"

Barbary scowled. "What?"

"You nodded — didn't you?"

"I guess so. What's so bad about that?"

"Nothing — except that up here you have to get out of the habit of nodding or shaking your head."

"Why?"

"Because the spin of the station affects your inner ear. That makes you feel like the floor is twisting or tilting, depending on which you're doing and what way you're facing. Go ahead — try it."

"Well . . . okay." She shook her head. The floor tilted up and back. Barbary stopped.

"Now turn this way" — Heather moved her a quarter turn — "and shake your head again."

This time it felt as if the floor were tilting from side to side.

"And if you turn around this way —"

"I don't like this very much." Barbary grabbed hold of the bunk support.

"But — oh. Oh, gee, Barbary, I didn't realize — here, sit down."

Barbary sat still, letting her equilibrium return. She tried to listen to Heather's explanation, but it was too much for her to take in all at once.

"You get so you don't notice it after a while," Heather said. "But by then most people have already trained themselves out of nodding or shaking their heads."

"That sounds like a good idea," Barbary said.

"Don't worry — you'll be an old hand in no time."

Mick jumped to the top bunk and curled up on Barbary's pillow.

"I think he's trying to tell us something," Heather said.

"Yeah," Barbary said. This time she did not nod.

When they had both lain down, and Mickey was purring beside Barbary, kneading her arm with his paws, Heather said, "Are you all settled?"

"Yeah."

"Lights out," Heather said.

The lights dimmed and went out.

A very long, very narrow triangle of light fell across the

70

floor. It came from the other room, through a crack where the door did not quite meet the wall.

Barbary had thought she was too nervous to sleep, but in the darkness and in the half-gravity ease of her bed, exhaustion began to take her over.

"Barbary?" Heather whispered.

Pulling herself partway out of a doze, Barbary answered. "Yeah?"

"Don't misunderstand — it's neat that you brought Mickey. But . . . how come you risked it?"

"I wanted to chase him away, but I couldn't. Then after we made friends, they wanted me to take him to the animal shelter so they could kill him."

"Oh," Heather said. "Oh. I'm glad you brought him."

I wonder how long I'm going to get away with it, though, Barbary thought.

"Heather?"

"Uh-huh?"

"How come you live here? In low gravity?"

Heather was silent, and Barbary thought she must have asked her something very rude.

But you asked me a personal question, Barbary thought. Don't I get a turn?

"Well," Heather said, "I have to. There's something wrong with my heart. I'm only allowed to go into one g a couple of hours a day."

"Oh," Barbary said. "I'm sorry."

"You don't need to be. I don't care. I like it here. I don't know why people want to stay at one g anyway."

She probably knew better than Barbary, who only knew

71

what the instruction book said. If people did not stay used to regular gravity, then after a long time in space it would be too hard for them to go back to earth.

As she drifted off to sleep, Barbary thought, But I don't want to go back to earth. I want to live in space, where there isn't any gravity.

Barbary flung her arm across her eyes to block out the sunlight —

There was no sunlight. She woke abruptly.

"Come on, kids," Yoshi said. "Dinnertime."

"Okay," Heather said. "Just a minute."

Barbary reached for Mickey. He was gone. She froze.

Yoshi had only made the lights go on; he had not come into the room or even opened the door very far. He closed it again.

"Heather!" Barbary whispered. "Mick's gone!" She flung off her blanket and searched her bunk and the bookcase, but the cat had disappeared.

"I'll get up in a minute."

The covers rustled as Heather turned over.

"Mick's gone!" She jumped off her bunk, but he was not curled up on a desk or a chair or in a corner or anywhere.

Heather sat up. "Did you look under the bed?"

Barbary knelt and lifted the edge of the comforter, then scowled at Heather in disgust.

"There isn't any 'under,' under the bed!" It was all drawers. "Will you wake up?"

"Uh-huh. Sure."

She flopped back down and pulled the comforter over her head. Barbary realized that Heather could carry on a conversation while she was still almost asleep.

"Heather!"

Heather yelped and flung aside the quilt.

"Jeez," Barbary said, "you don't need to be that way about it."

"I just found Mickey."

Mick curled sleeping in the middle of her bunk. He raised his head, yawned widely, his whiskers bristling, his tongue curling, put his head down again, and went back to sleep.

"Mick!" Barbary said. "You scared me to death." Mickey made no reply. "I thought he got out."

"Oh, he couldn't," Heather said. "Come on, let's get ready for dinner. I'm starved."

"Do we have to go?"

Heather glanced from Barbary to Mickey, and back again. "I know how you feel. I really do. But it'll look kind of strange if we don't go eat."

"I guess," Barbary said.

"And nobody will be here to find him."

Barbary chewed her thumbnail.

"Okay?" Heather said.

"Yeah," Barbary said, unconvinced.


The cafeteria on the half-g level contained only ten tables. Barbary wondered if the one-g level of the station had a larger cafeteria, where more people and more commotion would make pilfering food much easier. Barbary supposed,

73

though, that Heather must have to eat here most of the time.

"What do you want to eat?" Heather said, standing on tiptoe to see the top shelf.

"I don't know — what is there?"

"Chhay keeps threatening to import a herd of steers," Yoshi said, "but he hasn't got clearance for it —"

"Or a place to put it," Heather said.

"Anyway, there isn't any red meat," Yoshi said.

Barbary had never tasted beef.

"I didn't think of that," Heather said in a stricken voice. "Barbary, will it be okay? I mean —" She stopped.

Barbary realized that Heather meant, was there anything Mickey would eat. Mickey had never tasted beef either. Heather was going to have to learn to keep her mouth shut, or they were all going to be in a lot of trouble.

"Yeah, sure, it's okay."

Yoshi looked at them both oddly. "Heather, I'm sure Barbary doesn't expect everything to be just the same up here as back on earth."

"No, I don't," Barbary said. "I mean, it doesn't make any difference anyway. I never had any animal meat back there."

"Oh, good," Heather said, relieved. Barbary wondered if she had any idea how close she had come to letting too much information slip. Barbary knew Yoshi was suspicious, even if he did not yet know what to be suspicious of.

"How about some shrimp? They're surplus, from the ocean research project, so they're fresh."

Shrimp were even more of a luxury than beef, back on

74

earth, but Barbary had heard that cats liked them. She accepted the shrimp salad, even though the little pink curled-up things looked kind of disgusting. They would at least be easy to palm and hide in her napkin. Heather poured glasses of milk for herself and Barbary. The liquid flowed slowly and strangely in the low gravity. Barbary tried to think of a way to smuggle a glass of milk out of the cafeteria.

Maybe I can find a container with a lid, she thought, and sneak back later.

Heather chose a curry so hot that Barbary's nose prickled from the spices. Mick would never eat that, even if it weren't too squishy to take away, which it was.

Heather didn't bring a cat to a space station, Barbary told herself. It isn't her responsibility to feed him. It's yours.

They sat with several other people. Yoshi and Heather introduced Barbary to them and to friends at the surrounding tables. Roxane was a mechanic who worked outside the station, building new parts for it. Chhay was an agricultural expert. Ramchandra worked on computer components that could only be grown in weightlessness. He had helped to build the first picocomputer. He said organic computers were the coming thing, and that he would have to study biology if he wanted to keep up with his own field. Barbary did not know if he was joking or not. She managed to keep track of the people at their table, but could not remember everyone else's name. They all greeted her warmly and welcomed her to the station.

For the first time in as long as she could remember, Barbary began to believe she really belonged somewhere.

"When are you getting your dogies?" Heather said to Chhay. It sounded weird to Barbary, to hear in a space station a word from some old cowboy movie.

Chhay laughed, as if the herd of steers was an old joke between him and Heather. "Somehow I just can't seem to get that request approved," he said. "They're afraid the steers will get loose and overrun the station."

"Considering the birth rate of your average herd of steers," Roxane said, "no wonder pets aren't allowed."

Everybody laughed except Barbary, who had no idea what was so funny. Heather, who was taking a drink of milk, giggled right into her glass. Barbary used the distraction to palm a shrimp with the Murada technique. Her sleight of hand was only passable, but since no one was watching for her to fool them, and since they were all still laughing at the joke, she got away with it. Barbary had read about people no better at stage magic than she was, who had pretended to have special powers, real magic, and everyone believed them.

At the mention of pets, Heather stopped laughing and wiped off the splash of milk. She glanced at Barbary with a far-too-sober expression, calling attention to her just as she slipped the shrimp into her napkin.

Barbary frowned at Heather and pretended to be studying her salad. How were she and Mick ever going to get away with this? Heather had no experience at all at hiding things or lying, that was certain.

Ramchandra glanced at their table's single vacant chair. "Where's Thea?" he asked.

Barbary palmed another shrimp.

76

Yoshi shrugged. "Don't know," he said. He sounded disappointed. "In the observatory, probably. Working on the probe. Alien-watching. How's your salad, Barbary?"

She crumpled up her napkin in her lap. "Um, I haven't tasted it yet." She stuck her fork into it and pushed it around so no one would be able to tell how much was left. She hesitated, then gulped a shrimp.

"Hey," she said, surprised. "It's good."

"Eating one's first shrimp is an act of great courage," Roxane said, and everyone laughed. Barbary was ready to get angry, till she realized they were not laughing at her.

As soon as she had finished eating, Heather jumped to her feet and grabbed her tray. "Come on — I'll show you what to do with your stuff."

Barbary had to crush her napkin and shove it into her pocket before she could follow Heather. She caught up to her new sister on the other side of the cafeteria. A recess in the wall held racks for dirty dishes.

"You put the scraps over here. We make them into compost. Then —"

"Give me a little warning, will you?" Barbary muttered. "I had a lap full of shrimp."

"Oh, Barbary, I'm sorry, I didn't realize — I didn't see what you were doing."

"You weren't supposed to."

Heather picked up her plate and poked at the leftover curry sauce. "Should I get some chicken for him?"

"No, never mind, don't take anything."

"But —"

"You guys want anything? Tea?"

Barbary shut up as Chhay passed behind her. Heather opened her mouth to speak and Barbary glared at her to make her be quiet, but her sister surprised her. Heather scraped her leftovers down a narrow slide, then put her plate on a rack in a glass-fronted machine.

"After you clear off your dishes, you just stick them in here and when everybody's done we close the door and turn it on and sonic vibrations clean everything off. Tea would be great, Chhay."

Barbary turned around, trying to maintain her composure.

"Is there any coffee?"

"Sure." He poured a cup of coffee and put it on his tray, then looked over the selection of teas. "Heather, how about mint?"

"I think I'll have coffee, too," Heather said.

"Okay."

They returned to the table. Barbary wondered how long they had to stay at the table before they could excuse themselves.

Chhay put a tray full of steaming cups on the table. The steam acted strange in the low gravity. Barbary would have expected it to rise more quickly, but it collected in round clouds over the tray. Barbary discovered she could pull her cup right out from under its steam. But she was too concerned about Mick to wonder much or ask questions about anything else.

Barbary fidgeted. She kept expecting to be able to smell the soggy shrimp in her pocket.

Heather poured cream into her coffee till it was barely

78

even tan, then added sugar. Barbary liked coffee black, but if it tasted as bad as Heather thought, she would probably put stuff in it, too. She took a cautious sip.

Like all the other food aboard the station, the coffee tasted better than any Barbary had ever had before.

"Is Thea coming to the reception?" Roxane asked Yoshi.

"How should I know?" Yoshi said.

"Sorry," Roxane said. "Didn't mean to enter forbidden territory."

"I've barely seen her in a week." Yoshi turned his cup between his fingers. "Twenty hours a day at the telescope doesn't give her much time for the mundane things of life. Like talking to her lover or meeting a new member of his family."

He stared into his cup. His friends fell silent, then changed the subject. Heather's cheerfulness faded. Feeling uncomfortable, Barbary pretended not to notice. She had meant to ask Heather who Thea was, but she had forgotten. She was glad when, a few minutes later, Chhay stood up.

"We better hurry, or we'll be late."

All the others got up and put their dishes into the dishwasher.

"Okay," Chhay said. "Whose turn is it to wash them?"

"Not me," said Roxane. "I did it last time."

"This is stupid," Yoshi said. He slammed the dishwasher door, slapped the "on" button, and strode from the cafeteria. The dishwasher hummed and emitted a high-pitched whine that rose beyond the limits of human hearing.

Heather followed her father.

"Guess it was his turn," Roxane said dryly.

79

Barbary hurried after her sister.

"What was that all about?"

"It used to be a joke," Heather said. "Because it's so easy. Who washes the dishes just means who pushes the button. I guess . . . Yoshi doesn't feel much like joking today."

"He sounded sort of upset, earlier."

"Yeah. Because of Thea. They spend a lot of time together. Or anyway they did, till the spaceship appeared. Now, well, she's real busy. I mean, you can tell — she hasn't even had time to come meet you yet."

Barbary wished Heather would not put her in the middle of a disagreement between Yoshi and his lover. In her experience that was a dangerous place to be. She headed down the hallway toward the apartment.

"Wait, Barbary," Heather said. "This way."

"Is that a short-cut back to your place?"

"Unh-uh. This is the way to the reception hall."

Barbary stopped. "We're not going home?"

"Not till later."

The other adults passed. As they turned a corner, Chhay called back, "Come on, kids."

"Heather — " She waited till she was sure she could talk without being overheard. "What about Mick? I have to feed him. My pocket is all full of wet shrimp, and you said we could go back after dinner!"

"Oh, gee, I'm sorry — I meant after the reception. Besides, when you said not to take anything I thought you meant he wasn't very hungry."

"Oh. No. I just meant —" She almost said that if anybody had noticed Heather's pulling soggy bits of chicken out of her curry, it would have given them both away. But she did not want to hurt Heather's feelings. "I just meant you haven't had a chance to practice sleight of hand."

"Well, look, we can't go back now."

"He's going to be awful hungry."

"But it'll look too suspicious if we miss this party."

Yoshi returned.

"Are you two all right?"

"Sure," said Heather. "We're coming." She glanced at Barbary as if to say, See what I mean?

Barbary knew that if she kept behaving strangely, she would be sent back to earth. The friendship Yoshi had felt for her mother, twenty years before, would protect her only so far. She sighed and followed Heather. She tried to forget her pocketful of wet shrimp.

If I don't look at them, she said to herself, nobody else will, either . . .

# Chapter Seven

Heather and Barbary followed Yoshi to the one-g level of the station and into the reception hall.

"Wow," Heather said. "It's hot in here." She looked around. "Whoever's running balance on the station must be having a great time. I never saw so many people all in one place."

Barbary found the crowd neither large nor dense enough to bother her. Back on earth she had seen riots. Once she had even been caught at the edge of one. But Heather did not need to know about that experience. This crowd surrounded her with cheer and expectation, with eagerness to meet Jeanne Velory. Partitions lay fan-folded against the walls, pulled back to create a large meeting room from areas usually set aside for classes and lectures. All the chairs stood stacked in the corners, for the room did hold too many people for anybody to sit down.

Barbary and Heather made their way slowly through the crowd. Barbary could tell the station-dwellers from the grounders. About half the people here wore rather formal clothes, and the rest dressed like Heather and Yoshi, in T-shirts and drawstring shorts or pants. The grounders looked heavier, somehow, as if the one gravity of the station held them, while the station-dwellers seemed to bring with them the lower gravity of the inner ring. Barbary puzzled over the strange impression, because of course it was impossible. Gravity did not work that way. But that was how it looked to her even if she could not explain it, any more than she could explain the form the tea-steam took, or walking "down" an "up" grade, or the tilt of the elevator floor.

She wondered what she looked like herself: a grounder or — what *did* the people on the station call themselves? Atlanteans? Einsteinians? All the questions she wanted to ask tumbled over one another in her mind.

"Well. Barbary. Hello."

She started. Jeanne Velory gazed down at her, her expression pleasant, neutral, cool.

"Oh. Hi."

"Settling in all right?"

"Yes. Uh . . . thanks."

Heather nudged her. For the first three or four pokes in the ribs, Barbary had no idea why. Finally she figured it out.

"Jeanne, um, Dr. Velory. This is Heather. My new sister."

"How do you do, Heather." Jeanne shook Heather's small, slender hand. "We never were introduced, the last time I was here."

"No, I was just a kid then, anyway," Heather said.

"Have you shown Barbary the station yet?"

"We haven't had time. Tomorrow, I'm going to start."

Barbary blushed on being reminded that she had turned down Jeanne's offer of a guided tour around *Outrigger*.

"I saw the observation bubble," Barbary said. "In the transport ship. I found it myself. I stayed in it a lot. Nobody else was ever there."

Jeanne frowned, hearing the defensiveness in Barbary's voice, but her expression softened.

"I'm glad you found it," she said. "And you're right, hardly anyone else spent any time there. We wasted our time, instead. Arguing. We'd have done a lot better to look at the stars." She held out her hand to Heather again, then to Barbary. "I hope you like it here."

"Thanks," Barbary said.

"Dr. Velory . . ."

A tall man in a grounder suit touched Jeanne's shoulder. She let him turn her away to introduce her to a whole group of people, who closed in and cut her off from Barbary and Heather.

"You didn't tell me you knew her!" Heather said.

"I don't — we just sat next to each other on the shuttle. She knew who you are, though."

"Oh, yeah, big deal, everybody knows who I am, Heather the first space-baby. Really tiresome. I tell you, Barbary, it's great to have somebody else on the station who's under eighteen." She grinned. "Let's go get some punch. Maybe they even have a buffet . . . and you can give me a lesson in sleight of hand."

84

* *

The reception was a great success, but for Barbary it went on forever. Only when it began to break up did Heather think they could leave without attracting attention. Barbary had assumed they would be able to appear, then sneak off. Back on earth, no one ever cared if she disappeared. But Heather's absence would be noticed as much as her presence. Barbary began to see some of the drawbacks of Heather's life. She still envied her all the years she had spent up here — but she could see the drawbacks.

Now she followed Heather through the crowd. It was thinner, but still thick enough to make finding anyone a problem. Finally they saw Yoshi.

"I'm getting kind of tired," Heather said to him. "We're going to go on home."

"That's a good idea," Yoshi said. "I'll come with you."

Heather gave Barbary an anxious glance. Barbary took care not to react. She figured she had about one more chance at acting weird in front of Yoshi before he decided she was seriously nuts. Besides, even if he came back with them everything would be all right as long as he did not barge into Heather's room. And as long as Mick was not yowling at the top of his lungs when they got there.

Barbary had succeeded in forgetting about the shrimp until she started home. Just as the books on stage magic claimed, her ignoring something had kept others from noticing it. But as soon as she got on the elevator to the inner ring, she became uncomfortably aware of the damp handful of crus-

85

taceans in her pocket. And she thought she could smell them, too. She glanced sidelong at Yoshi, but he stared out at the stars, somewhere else entirely.

"What's that funny — Oh!" Heather stopped herself just as Barbary elbowed her in the ribs. "Ow!"

"What's the matter?" Yoshi was not too distracted to hear the protest in Heather's voice. "What's wrong? Are you two fighting?"

"Fighting?" Heather said. "No — why would we fight?"

"I thought you said, 'ow,' " Yoshi said to Heather, and to Barbary he said, frowning, "and I thought you hit her."

"Hit her!" Barbary said. "Why would I hit her?" She was offended. She would never hit Heather. Elbowing somebody in the ribs was not hitting them, and besides Heather was a lot smaller than she was. She had barely nudged her, and that only to get her attention.

"She didn't hit me!" Heather said, just as offended. "And I said 'oh' — I was thinking about something."

"I see," Yoshi said.

Barbary knew that Yoshi meant the opposite. Of course he could not see; how could he? She hoped he might put this whole day down to tiredness and excitement, and let her start fresh in the morning.

The elevator stopped. They all got out and turned the corner.

The door to Yoshi and Heather's apartment stood ajar.

Somehow, Barbary managed to keep walking. Her knees felt like oatmeal. Mick must have howled. Someone had heard him and found him and taken him away.

"Hmm," Yoshi said. "Thea must be here." He strode on ahead.

Heather grabbed Barbary's hand.

"It's okay," she whispered. "Thea wouldn't have any reason to go in our room."

They hurried after Yoshi.

He stood just inside the doorway, looking at a jumble of delicate bits of machinery and electronics spread across the living room floor. Heather stopped short. Barbary caught her breath.

Thea — Barbary assumed it was Thea — came out of Heather's room, leaving the door open.

Thea grinned. "Hi. You must be Barbary. Welcome to Atlantis." She waved something at Heather. "Heather, I borrowed your sticky tape. Hope that's okay."

"Uh . . ." Heather said. "Yeah, sure, anytime." Both she and Barbary stared at the door.

Barbary expected Mick to come sauntering through the doorway any second. But nothing happened.

Where *is* he? Barbary thought.

"Where've you all been?" Thea said, kneeling in the midst of the contraption.

"At the reception."

"The reception? Oh, lordy, the reception." Thea sat on her heels. "I thought that was Friday."

"It is. So is today."

Thea ran her hands over her light brown hair. A few strands fell free and curled around her face. "I must be losing my mind. I thought today was Wednesday."

"Thea, I'm worried about you," Yoshi said.

"Worried? Why?"

"You're usually only one day off."

Barbary would have been offended if someone said that to her. Thea took it in stride. Perhaps it was the truth.

"I wasn't paying attention — I have to get this thing finished. I need some floor space to put it together. That's okay, isn't it?"

Yoshi looked as if he had to decide whether to lose his temper or laugh. He chose laughter.

"Of course it is," he said. "And this way, I might even get to see you once in a while."

"Well," Heather said cheerily, "We'll leave you two alone. Time for bed." She grabbed Barbary by the hand, dragged her into the bedroom, and closed the door.

On the foot of the upper bunk, Mick sat with his paws curled under his chest. He blinked like an owl, and then he yawned.

Heather started to giggle.

"He must have been in the bookcase," Barbary said. "And just now come out —"

"Maybe," Heather said. "But I bet he was right where he is all along. Just watching the world go by."

"But Thea —"

"Watching Thea go by, too. You'll really like her, when you get to know her. She's great. When she's thinking about something, a bomb could go off right beside her and she'd never even notice it."

"Kind of dangerous," Barbary said.

"If there were any bombs around. But good luck for us."

Mick stood, stretched, and jumped to the floor. He sat at Barbary's feet, twitching his whiskers as he sniffed the air. She brought out the shrimp.

"This is disgusting," she said, peeling away bits of sodden paper napkin from the squashed and disintegrating shellfish. "I don't know if he'll even eat it."

But he did.

Barbary let Mick under her covers. He curled up next to her, purring and occupying at least half the bed. Barbary tickled him under the chin.

"We made it through a whole day, Mick," she whispered. "I don't know how, but we did."

He nuzzled her side and went to sleep. Barbary lay very still, marveling at the way half gravity felt, at her new family, at being here at all. A moment later, she fell asleep too.

When Barbary woke, Mick occupied three-quarters of the bunk instead of half. Barbary pushed herself into the corner formed by the mattress and the cool, solid wall. She tried to doze, but it was hopeless. She fished for her watch: five o'clock, station time. Most of the people on Atlantis kept to a regular 24-hour schedule, just because they were used to it and it was simpler to keep track of. Nobody would be up yet. Barbary's stomach growled. Last night, she had been so anxious to get food for Mickey that she had neglected to eat much herself.

She slipped out of her bunk, leaving Mick curled sleeping in its center. Perhaps Yoshi and Heather kept some food in their tiny kitchen, at least some milk that she could divide with Mick.

Heather slept on as Barbary got dressed. She lay so quiet, so still — Barbary remembered her sister's bad heart, and for a moment felt afraid. But when she listened, she could hear Heather's soft, shallow breathing.

Mick stuck his nose out from beneath the covers and mrrowed.

"Good morning." Barbary opened the door. Mick stood, ready to come exploring. "It's probably all right," Barbary whispered, "but just to be safe you better stay here." She slipped out.

"Hi."

Barbary spun around, frightened.

"Sorry," Thea said. "Didn't mean to scare you."

"Uh, that's okay." Barbary slid the door shut. "I didn't think anybody'd be up this early."

This morning, Thea's gadget looked more like a real machine than a collection of random parts.

"Most people aren't," she said.

"Have you been up all night?"

Thea looked at her watch. "Not quite — not yet, anyway." She grinned. "I figure I've got two or three hours to go before I can claim to've missed a whole night's sleep." She stood up and stretched. "Do you always get up this early?"

"No. Hardly ever."

"Is Heather awake?"

"Unh-uh — I mean," she said quickly to cover the conversation she had been having with Mick, in case Thea had heard, "she sort of turned over, so I said she should go back to sleep. I guess she did."

"She likes to sleep late, that's for sure," Thea said. "But once she gets going, there's no stopping her. Want some coffee?"

"Sure."

Thea poured two cups. Barbary sipped hers. Thea stared at her contraption.

"Is that a camera?" Barbary asked.

"A telescopic camera, yes."

"To look at the aliens with?"

Thea arched one eyebrow and regarded Barbary with approval. "That's right. The politicians have gummed up the works so nobody can go out and take a look at the thing in person — so I'm going to mount a camera on one of the rafts and send it on a grand tour."

"Is that allowed?"

"Everybody in the astronomy department knows about it — but if the muck-de-mucks knew, they'd probably forbid it. Saying no is easier than saying okay. They've already taken over all the information from the other probe I sent out — the one that detected the alien ship in the first place." She gestured toward the series of comet photos Barbary had noticed the previous evening. This was the first chance Barbary had had to look at them.

The first two photos showed an ordinary comet, a blurry streak against the stars. But in the third photo, the spot of light had become clearer and sharper. A real comet grew fuzzier with vaporized ice as it approached the sun.

Barbary stared at the last two photos.

The images Thea had captured could not be mistaken for a chunk of rock or ice, even less for a human creation. The alien ship sprawled in all dimensions, flowing out in angles and curves that no one on earth ever imagined for a spacecraft. It was exquisitely beautiful and exquisitely alien.

"I'm supposed to be an astronomer and this is supposed to be a research station," Thea said. "But now that we have something to research, the politicians are getting all nervous."

"That's crummy," Barbary said.

"That's what I thought. So it's guerrilla time."

"Gorilla time?"

"Guerrilla, as in warfare. That's when you go around behind somebody else's rules, especially if the rules don't make sense."

"I hope it works."

"So do I. By the time the ship gets in visual range — close enough to see details, I mean — the VIPs will probably try to lock up all the light telescopes as well as the probe data. I don't see how they can, though. It'd be like trying to take away every computer in the station. Practically everybody has one."

"Why would they try, then?"

"Fear."

"It seems like they'd want to know all they can find out before the ship gets here."

"They have tame scientists to tell them what they want to know. They can't figure the rest of us out, and they're afraid we might tell them something that doesn't fit in with their pet theories."

"Like what?"

Thea paused, then shrugged and gestured to her camera. "When I get a transmission from this bird, I'll let you know."

The look on Thea's face reminded Barbary of Jeanne, when Jeanne had said, "A lot of people think the alien ship is a derelict. I don't believe it, myself."


Heather sat on the top bunk, skritching Mick behind the ears.

"But it would be too suspicious to tell Thea to stay out of our room, Barbary. Besides, what would she think? I'd hurt her feelings."

"But she shouldn't just walk in. What would she say, if you walked right into her room?"

"Probably, 'Hi, sit down, have a cup of coffee.' "

"Oh."

"Honest, Barbary, she hardly ever comes in here. She never has before and she probably won't ever again. It was just a fluke. Mick will be okay."

"I guess." She tired to persuade herself that Heather was right.

"If you're worried about him, why don't you bring him with us?"

"I can't, he'd never sit still for it."

"But you could put him in your jacket, in the hidden pocket."

"He wouldn't stay. He only stayed before because I drugged him."

"Oh." Heather rested her chin on her fist and frowned. "How about a briefcase?"

"What's a briefcase?"

"It's a big leather satchel people used to carry papers around in."

"Why'd they do that?"

"They didn't have computers. They had to write everything down. In this novel I read, the hero carried his cat around in a briefcase."

"Maybe you could train some cats to do that," Barbary said, "but I don't think Mick would like it. And where would we get a briefcase, anyway?"

"It's the principle of the thing. We could use a box."

"We'd look pretty stupid walking around the station carrying a box with airholes punched in the side."

"Maybe so," Heather said. "But I can't think of anything else."

"He's fed and everything. He'll probably just sleep all morning anyway. He'll be okay. It's just . . ."

"What?"

"After a while he's going to get bored with this one room. He'll want to run around. If he could do that, someplace where nobody else would see —"

"There's lots of places nobody ever goes but me. Sometimes I think I'm the only one who even knows about them. I'll show them to you. But first I want to take you for a ride."

Barbary skritched Mick behind the ears. He barely raised

his head, his eyes closed, then he put one paw over his face and fell asleep.

As the elevator rose toward the zero-gravity hub, Barbary and Heather watched the stars through the clear wall of the elevator.

"They're even prettier when you get outside the station and you're just in a suit or a raft," Heather said. "Sometimes I think it ought to be possible to go outside without a suit, and see them without anything at all in the way."

Barbary glanced at her sister, trying to figure out if Heather was making a joke. If she was, it was not a very good one. Barbary had never felt scared for another person before. She felt scared for Heather.

"It'd be kind of cold out there, without a space suit," she said.

Heather grinned. "Or really hot. Depends on where you're standing."

The elevator stopped and opened. Heather grabbed Barbary and pushed off, soaring across the room. She slyed around the hub. On one side, a number of small spacecraft sat on rails, facing closed hatches in the wall.

"Yukiko, hi, can I take one of the rafts?"

Yukiko straightened from her inspection of a raft's engines. She carried a torqueless wrench in one hand; a bunch of other tools hung from a sort of apron tied around her waist. She was tiny, only a bit taller than Heather.

"Hi, Heather," she said.

"Yukiko, this is Barbary."

"Hello, Barbary. I heard you were coming. Welcome to Atlantis."

"Thanks." Being recognized everywhere she went felt weird. She supposed she would get used to it.

"I'll just take my regular raft, okay?" Heather headed toward a blue-gray ship.

"Sure," Yukiko said. "Have fun. Oh — want to do an errand?"

"Okay. What goes where, and who to?"

Yukiko unfastened a great netted bundle of equipment from the wall and floated it to Heather's raft. She reached inside the passenger compartment and manipulated some controls. Crab-clawed arms reached out from the raft's belly and clasped the bundle close.

"Sasha needs it, out on the platform."

Heather slid into the raft and showed Barbary how to strap in.

"See you later."

Heather sealed the clear canopy.

"Let's go," she said.

The raft glided forward on its rails. The hatch opened, let them pass, and shut behind them. The raft stopped before a second closed hatch. Air hissed loudly as the air lock emptied. The sound diminished to silence.

"Is it like the light switch?" Barbary said. "You work it by talking to it?"

"Right," Heather said. "You can use hand controls, too, I'll show you. And you should keep an eye on the gauges, too, just in case something goes wrong." She pointed to one lighted display. "This one's for air pressure, so you know the canopy's properly sealed. And if anything does happen, there's a survival sack right there." She pointed to a silvered package in easy reach. "You just open it and seal it around you. It's got its own air supply and an emergency transmitter, and even a window."

"Is there time to get into it? I mean, if a meteor hits the raft, or something?"

Heather laughed. "If a meteor hit us we'd be vaporized. You wouldn't have time to get in the sack, but you wouldn't have time to care, either. The chances of getting hit by a meteor are real low. Around here we're more likely to run into a loose wrench."

The gauge displaying air pressure outside the raft dropped to zero. The outer hatch opened. Heather put her hands on the controls.

"You can make it work by telling it how fast you want to be going, but once you get a feeling for it, it's more fun to drive it."

The raft slid forward, left its rails, and sailed off into space. All of a sudden they were completely free.

Now Barbary understood why they called the little spaceships "rafts." She could tell that they were moving because the station fell away behind them, and the acceleration pressed her against her seat, but the motion gave her no perception of speed, no sound of air rushing by or wheels on pavement, just a smooth, peaceful, floating sensation as if they were drifting down a dark, wide river.

"They really let you take this out all by yourself," Barbary said with wonder.

"Sure."

"They don't let kids drive cars, back on earth."

"That's dumb. Why not?"

"They don't think we're responsible enough, I guess."

"Hmph," Heather said, offended. "I've never had an accident. I never got drunk and took a raft out to race and nearly ran into the transport, like somebody I could name. And I've never run out of fuel, either. It's adults who do that. Not kids."

"But you're not a regular kid."

"I am too! What do you mean by that?"

"I mean —" Barbary tried to say exactly what she did mean. "I mean you're different from most of the other kids I've ever met. They're all kind of silly, and, I don't know, bored."

"I get bored sometimes. I can be as silly as anybody, too. Want to see?"

The steering rockets vibrated. The raft spun on its long axis and whipped back to front to back at the same time. The stars and the station spiraled past. Barbary squeezed her eyes shut.

When she looked again, the raft sailed in a perfectly straight line, as if it had never departed from its course. Satisfied and unperturbed, Heather drove on. Barbary felt as if she were still spinning. She clapped her hands over her ears, shut her eyes, and buried her face against her knees.

"I meant it as a compliment!" she said.

"Oh," Heather said. She patted Barbary's shoulder. "I'm sorry. But I hate it when people give me that, 'Oh, isn't she mature?' stuff. I feel like they expect me to die any minute."

"I still meant it as a compliment."

"Okay. I believe you. Come on, Barbary, sit up, you've got to get used to ignoring what your balance tells you sometimes. You sort of have to rely on your eyes."

Barbary raised her head. The dizziness faded.

"I guess," she said, "it *could* get to be fun . . ."

"Yeah," Heather said. "Shall I do it again?"

"Not quite yet," Barbary said with her teeth clenched.

"Okay. I'm not actually supposed to, this close to the station. Besides, we'll be at the construction site in a minute."

"Where is it?"

"Just there." Heather pointed straight ahead at a cluster of stars.

"But —"

Sunlight touched one edge of a curve of metal. Barbary gasped. As the observation platform and the space station moved in their orbits around each other, the shadow of the station slipped away, leaving the delicate platform in full sunlight.

"It's so small," Barbary said.

"No, it isn't. It's huge. Look, you can just see one of the workers."

"Where?" Barbary expected someone in a space suit to appear and scoop up the filigree sphere of the platform like a basketball.

"There. To the left."

"I don't see anything."

"We're still a couple of kilometers from it."

The clarity of space had tripped Barbary up. She saw that

99

she had mistaken something far away but distinct for something close. Now she could not estimate the platform's size at all. It grew larger and larger. By the time Barbary spotted the worker who floated deep within the spindly struts and braces, the person was the size of a doll instead of the size of a speck. The platform dwarfed the raft.

"Hi, Heather," said a disembodied voice.

Barbary started, then realized that the voice had come over the radio. A space-suited figure made its way out of the interior of the platform and floated just outside. She looked "up" at them while they looked "up" at her. Barbary felt very weird.

"Hi, Sasha. This is Barbary."

Sasha raised the reflective visor of her helmet. She moved closer to the raft's bubble and cupped her gloved hands around her faceplate so Barbary could see her. A yellow headband, bright against her dark skin, restrained her curly black hair.

"Welcome to Atlantis, Barbary." She had a wonderful, soft accent that Barbary could not place, sort of British, sort of Russian.

"Thanks."

"Are you coming out?"

"Not this time," Heather said. "I didn't bring any suits. I just wanted to show Barbary how the raft works."

Sasha chuckled. "Yes. I saw your demonstration."

Heather blushed. "I had to dodge a wrench," she said.

"Or a foo-fighter?"

Heather grinned. "Sure. Didn't you see it? I bet it was a spy from the alien ship."

"When you see it again, tell those little green people to stop in for tea," Sasha said. "Well. Got to get back to work." She made a graceful dive to the other side of the raft, where a couple of her co-workers joined her. Heather extended the arms of the raft. The equipment clanged, startling Barbary all over again.

"Thanks, kids," Sasha said, waving, as she helped tow the equipment over to the platform. "On the way back, don't hit any of those little green pedestrians."

Heather turned the raft end-for-end and headed home. Going back they were upside-down, compared to the way they had arrived, but after a moment it no longer *felt* upside-down to Barbary.

"What's a foo-fighter?"

"It's what pilots used to call UFOs — flying saucers — years and years ago, before anybody ever went into space. Some people thought they were alien spaceships coming to contact us, or spy on us, or take over our world, or give us the secrets of the universe. Or something."

"Does that make the alien ship a foo-fighter?"

After a thoughtful pause, Heather said, "I guess it does. But nobody ever found any hard evidence that the old UFOs were real. This one's kind of different."

Heather piloted the raft smoothly into its bay and the airlock began its cycle.

"That was fun," Barbary said. She still felt dizzy — but the ride *had* been fun. "How long does it take to learn to drive one of these things?"

"Anybody can get in one and ride around in it," Heather

said. "But really driving it, with the computer overridden — I don't know. I've been doing it since I was a little kid."

"How long does it take other people?"

"Couple months, I guess. Mostly they just let the computer do it. It's more fun to drive it, though. Next time I'll give you a lesson."

"Great."

The airlock completed its cycle and the raft slid into the station. Heather opened the canopy and vaulted from her seat. Barbary followed, still uncertain in free fall.

"Thanks, Heather, Barbary," Yukiko said.

"Any time."

Heather led Barbary from the hub.

"What do you want to see next?" she asked. "The labs are pretty neat, and the library — or we could play on the computer —"

"I ought to go check on Mickey," Barbary said.

"Oh, I'm sure he's okay."

"Heather —" Barbary said, exasperated. She stopped for a second to make herself calm down. "I know you want to show me everything, and I want to see it. But Mick's my responsibility. I have to take care of him and be sure he's all right. Otherwise I just should have let him loose back on earth where he'd have half a chance without me."

Heather walked along in silence for quite a way. Barbary felt certain that her new sister was angry at her. She did not know Heather well enough to know how she would react when she got mad.

"Yeah," Heather said, to Barbary's surprise. "Yeah, you're

right. I understand. I hadn't really thought about it enough, but I see what you mean. You have to protect him. And I'm going to help you."

# Chapter Eight

Closer to completion, Thea's contraption sat on the living room floor. Thea had fallen asleep on the couch. The door to Heather's room remained tight shut. Barbary slid it open.

"Lights," Heather said.

"Hey, Mick," Barbary whispered.

He made the squeaky-purring sound he always made when he woke. From the storage shelf of the upper bunk he yawned and blinked at her. He rose, stretched, and suddenly jumped for the door. Barbary caught him. He turned in her hands and attacked her fingers, partly in fun, but partly in earnest.

"He's bored," Barbary said. "He's really bored. He hardly ever bites." She tussled with him, letting him fight with her hand even when he got excited and stuck his claws into her. But he would never get enough exercise pouncing on her hand. "He used to spend just about all night outside, even though it was dangerous. What am I going to do, Heather?"

"He needs a place where he can run around, huh?"

"Yeah. But a really private place."

Heather sat on top of her desk and leaned her chin on her hand.

"I know where to go," she said. "Only we have to get him there. Can you try to hide him in your jacket?"

"*Sometimes* he'll lie still for a little while. Not long, though. Can we go a way that not very many people use? Just in case?"

"We'll have to," Heather said, and jumped up before Barbary could ask what she meant by that. "Where'd you put your jacket?"


Mick crouched in the secret pocket, but Barbary knew he would want to get out soon. She followed Heather along one of the corridors that curved around the inner surface of the station's wheel.

"Heather," Barbary said, "am I just imagining it, or does walking feel different depending on which direction you're going?"

"It really is different. Because of the spin."

"I don't understand."

"Okay. You've got weight here because of the spin, right?"

"Uh-huh."

"So if you walk plus-spin — that's the same direction the station's spinning — you're going even faster than the station. Since your weight is proportional to your speed, you feel heavier. And it makes you feel kind of like you're walking uphill. That's why when you see people jogging in the

105

one-g level, they usually run plus-spin. They get their exercise faster."

"I guess I understand."

"Then if you go the opposite way, minus-spin" — Heather turned and ran a few steps in the opposite direction — "you subtract your speed from the station's speed. That makes you feel lighter. And you think maybe you're going downhill."

"It's weird," Barbary said.

"No, it isn't!" Heather said. "Oh . . . I guess it is. But you'll get used to it. You can feel it even more if you run. Go ahead, try it."

Mickey squirmed, trying to escape.

"I will later," Barbary said. "But if I run now, Mick will have a fit. How much farther do we have to go?" She put her hand on the outside of the secret pocket and tried to pet Mick to calm him down and hold him still at the same time.

"To the bottom of the elevator."

Inside the elevator, Heather opened a panel, pushed a button marked −3, and slid the panel shut. None of the usual numbers lit up, but they descended. Barbary leaned against the wall where the outlines were painted, hoping she would soon get used to the tilt when the elevator moved.

Barbary opened her jacket. Mick stuck his head out of the pocket. He looked ready to jump any second.

"Stay there, Mick!" she said.

"Hardly anybody ever uses this elevator," Heather said. "He's safe now."

"Maybe I could let him out?"

"Probably it'd be all right, but we'll be where we're going in a minute."

The elevator slowed and stopped.

"Oh, no!" Heather said.

Barbary flung her jacket closed, hugging it to her with her hand still inside. Mickey pressed his head against her fingers.

Jeanne Velory and Ambassador Begay got into the elevator.

"Hello, Barbary. Hello, Heather," Jeanne said.

"Hi." Mick's cold nose and prickly whiskers tickled her as he nudged around looking for a way out. "Uh —"

"Hi," Heather said, detecting the note of desperation. "I'm showing Barbary around. We already went on a raft ride to the observation platform."

"We haven't had a chance to see the observation platform from up close yet," Jeanne said. "You've got a good guide, Barbary."

"I know," Barbary said.

"But aren't you hot in your jacket?"

As Barbary tried to think of an answer, Mick hooked his claws around her wrist.

"You're Ambassador Begay, aren't you?" Heather said.

"Yes, I am."

Jeanne introduced Heather and Barbary to the ambassador, and for a horrible moment Barbary thought she would have to shake hands, when it was her right hand inside her jacket holding Mickey still.

But Heather broke in. "Later on I'm going to show Barbary the computer." Her voice sounded a little too high and

107

a little too loud. "It has some great games. Have you tried 'Snarks and Boojums'? It's really fun."

You're really overdoing it, Heather, Barbary thought, willing the elevator to stop and open, willing Jeanne to get bored with talking to two kids, willing the electricity to go out, *anything*. All the attention was on her and Heather — mostly on Heather; she had to admit that her sister did a good job of keeping attention off Barbary and Mick — and the whole business was like a scene out of a sappy kids' movie. "The Space Colony Children" or something. Ugh, Barbary thought, aren't we cute. Mick, if you don't stop biting me I'm going to let you get out, and see what happens then.

"I haven't had time to do that yet, either," Jeanne said.

"You ought to," Heather said. "It's got a lot of physics in it. The computer's terrific. You can even make up stories on it."

"What tales does your computer tell you?" Ambassador Begay asked.

"You tell it your name and it sort of puts you into the story. It never tells the same one twice."

"I see. The stories I know do not change at all. But perhaps you'll let me tell you one anyway, if we can find the time."

"I'd like that," Heather said.

Barbary struggled to remain expressionless as Mick dug his claws into her hand.

"Barbary, is your hand all right?" Jeanne said.

The elevator slowed and stopped and the door slid open. But nobody moved.

"Yes," Barbary said. "Why shouldn't it be? I mean . . .
um . . . I'm just pretending to be Napoleon. It's part of the
story."

She looked at Heather and Heather looked at her and
neither one of them could help it. They both burst out
laughing. Jeanne watched them quizzically, then stepped
outside. Ambassador Begay followed.

"Getting off?"

"Unh-uh," Heather said, gasping for breath. "We're just
riding the elevator. We wanted to come to the bottom and
go right back up." She caught Barbary's gaze, and they both
laughed even harder.

"Okay," Jeanne said. "Have fun."

As she and the ambassador walked away, Heather lunged
forward and jammed her thumb against the "close door"
button. As soon as they were safe, she slid to the floor,
giggling.

"Nobody ever comes on this elevator, huh?" Barbary said.

"Napoleon!" Heather said. "Napoleon? That was great!"

"Mickey, ouch, stop it, all right, get down if you have to,
and if they throw you out the airlock it isn't my fault!" She
loosed her hold on the cat and he sprang to the floor. Barbary slid down beside Heather. "Napoleon. Good grief. What
a dumb thing to say. Now Jeanne must really think I'm an
idiot."

The elevator halted. Barbary grabbed Mick before the doors
opened. She carried him out into just about the weirdest
place she had ever seen.

The elevator sat on top of a wide platform. Steps led down
on all sides, making it into a ziggurat shape, a stepped pyr-

109

amid. About twenty steps below, the stairs disappeared into great piles of dirt and rocks, which rose to meet the curved horizon. Support beams projected through the dirt.

Mick scrabbled at Barbary's hands, caught his back claws against her palms, and leaped from her grasp. She yelped in surprise and pain. He ran across the platform, down the stairs, and over a hillock into the shadows.

"Mick!"

Barbary chased him, but Mick's rabbity rump vanished into the darkness before she reached the bottom of the stairs. She stopped and put her scratched hand to her mouth. The scratches stung.

"Mick!"

Barbary's eyes became accustomed to the eerie light cast by the fluorescent tubes on the ceiling. A few marks around the platform might have been small footprints, but they looked as if a wind had disturbed and blurred them. Mickey's tracks led across them and vanished.

"Mick!"

"It's okay," Heather said. "There's no place he can go, and nobody ever, ever comes down here. Not even me, mostly."

"That's what you said about the elevator."

"I said 'hardly ever' about the elevator. It leads to other places. But this is the lowest level of the station. It's the insulation against cosmic rays and solar flares. There isn't any reason for anybody to come down here. All it is is pulverized moon rock."

"Moon rock?" At the bottom of the stairs, Barbary poked

at the moon rocks with the toe of her shoe. "It looks like just dirt."

"It is," Heather said. "It's a good radiation shield, though, and once they finished the mass-driver on the moon, it was cheap. The mass-driver throws moon rocks out here into orbit, you catch them and extract whatever you want that's useful, then you put the leftovers here. This place is sort of a dump, to tell you the truth. But it makes the station safe to live in."

The crushed moon rock felt like ordinary, fine, dry dirt. Barbary's shoe left an impression just behind Mick's first pawprint.

"I never stepped on dirt from the moon before," Barbary said.

Heather grinned. "Maybe someday we'll get a chance to step on moon dust when it's still on the moon. Come on, I'll show you around."

Heather set off after Mickey. She walked more slowly than usual. Barbary remembered that her sister spent little time in full gravity. Barbary, too, felt the change in gravity even after such a short time of living on the middle level. She felt heavier than back on earth. She halted, but the heavy feeling remained. It was more than the effect of walking plus-spin. Then she realized that the lowest level really did have a greater acceleration than the one-gravity level just above. It might not be enough greater for her to feel it, but she *thought* she did.

The moon dirt filled the level with a long series of low hills. As far as Barbary could see, till the rising horizon disappeared beneath the roof, the ground rose and fell regularly.

"Why did they fill it with hills?" Barbary asked. The spooky, silent dimness made her whisper.

"They didn't," Heather said in a normal tone that sounded so loud Barbary almost jumped. "When I found it, a few years ago, the surface was flat. Kind of irregular, but mostly flat. Then — it changed. I don't know what formed the hills and valleys. Some kind of resonance with the spin, I guess, but I haven't figured out how to calculate it yet."

"What does everybody else think?"

Heather reached the top of one of the hills and paused, trying to pretend her breathing came easily. Her forehead gleamed with sweat. Barbary wondered if she should try to persuade Heather to go back upstairs before they found Mick. But she decided she had better not, at least not yet.

"I don't think anybody else knows about the hills," Heather said. "They're all so busy . . . I've only come down here five or six times. And . . . I never told anybody, because I figured they'd say I have to stay out. So I can't very well ask."

"I guess not," Barbary said.

Here and there a fluorescent light had burned out, further dimming the low illumination. Barbary had to squint to see much at all. She walked down a hill, following Mickey's tracks.

"How did you find out about this place?" she asked.

"I've explored everywhere," Heather said. "I realized when I was pretty little that you couldn't get to a lot of places

112

without doing something special, so I started looking for the special ways."

"Like the extra panel in the elevator."

"Uh-huh."

"Are all the other places as spooky as this one?"

Heather laughed. The cheerful sound lightened the dim atmosphere.

"No. This is the spookiest. Most places aren't exactly hidden, they're just out of the way. Like the ventilators and the recyclers."

Mick's tracks led into the valley between two hillocks and up the side of a third rise. Barbary glanced back. Her footprints made clear indentations in the dirt, but the elevator island had nearly vanished between the low ceiling and the tops of the hills.

"How fast does the dirt change?" she asked. "I mean — will our footprints disappear?"

"No," Heather said. "In a couple months they'll fade away. But we can't get lost even if they did vanish. There's more than one elevator, so even if you got turned around, you'd find your way out eventually."

"Mick!" Barbary called, in a soft voice. "Kitty, kitty!"

"Won't he come back to you?"

Abashed, Barbary stopped calling him. "He always has before," she said. "Except, he does it when he wants to, not always when you want him to." She had no good reason for feeling so uncertain about him.

"He'll be okay," Heather said. "He's only been gone a few minutes."

"I just hope he doesn't think he can stay out all night, like he did back on earth," Barbary said. "If he does, we might be here for a while."

Heather started to say something, but stopped. Before Barbary could ask what was the matter, Heather changed the topic.

"Come on," she said. "We can follow Mick's tracks so we'll be close to him when he does decide to come back."

"They ought to plant grass or something," Barbary said. The bare hillocks extended as far as she could see. "Then you'd have a park. It might be kind of pretty."

"That's a good idea," Heather said. "It really is! It would be sort of like being in one of the colonies. They'd have to change the lights . . ." She glanced around, as if imagining grass, flowers, trees.

She reached the top of a rise and stopped, breathing harder. Barbary felt as if she'd taken a slow walk around the block.

"You better go upstairs," Barbary said. "You've been down here kind of a long time, I'll stay and find Mick —"

"I'm okay, Barbary," Heather said. "I'm supposed to spend *some* time at one g, and usually I don't get around to it, so it's good that I'm here."

"But if Mick decides to hide out for a couple of hours —"

"We might have to go home for a while and come back and get him later."

Barbary said nothing. She did not want to leave Mick here. Probably it was much safer than being out on the street at night back on earth. But still she did not want to leave him here.

Barbary and Heather tramped on across the small hills

114

and valleys, following Mick's faint pawprints. He had scampered back and forth, sprinting one way, then the other, stopping, hurtling off in another direction. Barbary wished she had seen him, because he was fun to watch when he played like that.

They followed his tracks for a long way. The elevator had long ago vanished above the horizon, so everything looked exactly the same in every direction.

"I know we can't get lost," she said. "But it sure is strange down here."

"Yeah," Heather said. Her voice was very soft. Barbary could not tell in this light if her sister looked pale, but she was definitely sweating.

"Maybe you'd better rest," Barbary said.

"No, I'm okay, honest."

Suddenly her knees collapsed and she sat down hard in the dirt.

"Heather!"

"Well, I will be," Heather said, sounding disgusted. "In a minute."

"Come on, I'm going to get you back to the elevator."

Heather fended off her help. "I just want to sit here for a while."

"You've got to get out of this gravity — I bet I can carry you piggyback."

"What's piggyback?" Heather asked skeptically.

"You sort of sit on my back and I put my hands under your knees . . ."

It was easier to show her than tell her, so she did. Heather felt light and frail when Barbary picked her up.

115

"Now just wrap your arms around my neck. Only try not to strangle me."

Heather hugged herself against Barbary's back. As she reached around to hold on, her hand brushed Barbary's bare throat.

"Jeez, your hands are cold!" Barbary said. "Do you want to wear my jacket?"

"Unh-uh," Heather said. "My hands are always cold. Honest. I'll be okay."

But her voice was so feathery and weak that Barbary felt afraid. She turned back to retrace her footsteps, for she was no longer certain in which direction the elevator lay.

"Wait, Barbary, there's a different elevator the same way we were going. It's nearer than the other one. And maybe we'll find Mick."

"Okay."

Barbary trotted over the hillocks, following Heather's directions, now and then crossing Mick's track. Soon the base of a second elevator platform sank from the horizon as they neared it. Mick's pawprints led right to it, but she could not see Mick.

Barbary climbed the steps and let Heather down.

"How are you feeling?"

"Better," Heather said. "That was kind of fun."

Barbary grinned. Heather did look better now. She hoped it was not just because the light was brighter.

"You get the elevator," Barbary said. "I'll see if maybe Mick is on the other side."

She ran down the stairs two at a time. Mick's trail circled

the platform, then led onto the first step. She found a faint dusty pawprint. She climbed the stairs, calling him. But he was not at the top of the platform behind the elevator, or on either side.

"Heather," she called, "did Mick come around that way?"

"No, I haven't seen him. But the elevator's here. I can't keep it very long, somebody might get suspicious."

"I can't *find* him," Barbary said.

"I'll let it go for now."

"Go on up. I'll come in a while." Before Heather could reply, Barbary returned to the lowest step and followed it all around the square base. But the only pawprints were those she had already found. No prints led away from the platform. She turned, hoping to see Mick behind her, sneaking up like a character in some slapstick comedy. Barbary did not feel much like laughing. Besides, he was not there.

The only place Mick could have hidden was on the elevator. Somehow it must have arrived before Barbary and Heather, then it opened, then he got in, and now he was loose in the ship for anybody to discover. Barbary ran up the steps, panting. She reached the closed elevator door. Heather was nowhere to be seen. She must have gone home. Barbary pushed the elevator panel, pressing her hand against its lighted surface as if her intensity could make it return faster.

Maybe somehow she had missed seeing him. She ran to the corner of the elevator housing and looked beyond its edge. She saw nothing. She ran past the elevator doors and glanced down that side of the platform.

117

Heather stared at the wall.

"Heather, what's wrong? You were supposed to go back up!"

"You better come here," Heather said.

Barbary joined her.

An access panel lay askew, hanging by one fastener from the wall of the elevator housing. The hole it was supposed to close was only partly covered. The panel left open a triangular space more than big enough for a small cat to crawl into.

Barbary grabbed the panel and jerked it aside, bending it at the corner. Metal screeched on metal. She reached into the hole, but Heather grabbed her arm.

"Don't! I don't know what you'd touch, but probably electric wire and maybe the elevator cables, too. You might get electrocuted, or lose a finger, or something."

Barbary heard the faint vibration as the elevator slid toward them.

"But Mick's in there!" she cried. "I've got to get him out!"

"Wouldn't he meow or something? I don't hear anything."

"Where else could he be? What if he's hurt? If I could get electrocuted or squashed, so could he!"

"Try calling him."

Barbary bent close to the opening. "Hey, Mick! Kitty, kitty, kitty!"

She heard only the approach of the elevator.

"Can't we stop it?"

"No."

"But what if Mick's underneath it?"

The elevator's vibration slowed and stopped. Barbary cringed, expecting to hear a yowl of pain, imagining Mick crouched terrified under the falling cage. But she heard nothing but the soft slide of doors opening. She started to shiver.

"We've got to do something!"

Heather climbed to her feet, staring at the hole.

"Does he have a good sense of smell?"

"Not very. But some. Oh! If we get some food and put it here, he might smell it."

"Right." Heather hurried around the corner and caught the doors just before they closed. "Come on."

"I don't want to leave him here."

"It's the only choice," Heather said.

Barbary felt like crying. "What if it doesn't work?"

"Then," Heather said, "we'll have to get some help. We'll have to admit we came down here. And . . ."

"I'll have to admit Mick's in the station," Barbary said.

# Chapter Nine

On the way up, the elevator remained as deserted as Heather had said it ought to be on the way down. When Heather and Barbary got out at the half-g level, Heather just stood there for a couple of minutes. Barbary waited, anxious about Mick, but equally worried about Heather.

"I'm okay, honest," Heather said. "Let's go." She headed toward the apartment, trying to cheer Barbary up until Barbary wanted to scream.

I never should have let Mick get out of sight, she thought.

"We could go get him some shrimp," Heather said. "He liked that pretty well, didn't he?"

"Yeah," Barbary said. "But it doesn't smell very strong. I think I better use the stuff I brought with me. It smells awful. But Mick likes it."

"Okay."

They entered the apartment. Thea had awakened from her nap. She sat on the floor working on her contraption, and Yoshi sat on the couch reading a book. Yoshi glanced up, but Thea continued to tinker with a delicate bit of machinery.

"Hi, kids," Yoshi said.

"Hi," Heather said. "I'm still showing Barbary around — we just came back to get something we forgot."

She headed for her room.

"What have you seen so far?"

Barbary started to tell Yoshi about the raft trip, but changed her mind. What if Heather had persuaded the other adults to let her take the raft out by herself, but had never told her father? The raft might be nearly as much a secret as the shield level. She needed to talk to Heather about exactly what was safe to tell adults around here, and what wasn't.

"Oh, we've been all over. We talked to Jeanne Velory, and Ambassador Begay," she said, hoping to distract him from details.

"Did you see the gardens?"

"The gardens?" Barbary tried to remember what Heather had told her about the gardens.

"Your shoes are dirty," he said. "It's elementary, my dear Watson."

Barbary felt confused. Yoshi laughed.

"You read too many Sherlock Holmes books," Heather said.

"I know, but I couldn't resist. It seemed a safe bet, though — the gardens are the only place on the ship where you can get dirt on your shoes."

Thea glanced up as if she were about to say something,

121

then drew her eyebrows together and bent over her gizmo again.

"I took Barbary on a raft trip — we did an errand for Yukiko," Heather said. "We're going right back out again."

"Not till after you've rested for a while."

"But, Yoshi —"

"No arguments," he said. "I know you're excited about showing Barbary around. But there's plenty of time. You don't need to neglect your health. You can't neglect your lessons much longer, either."

Heather glared at him, then turned and stomped off into her bedroom. She and Yoshi must have had this argument before; Heather must know she could not win it.

"It's hard," Yoshi said, "to strike a balance between restricting her and letting her run herself ragged."

"I understand," Barbary said. "I don't want her to do anything that will make her sick. Honest."

"I'm glad. She can do anything she wants — I don't ever want her to start being afraid she can't. She just can't do it all at once. None of us can, but sometimes it's hard to convince Heather of that."

"I'll just go and tell her not to be mad or anything, then come right out and — and go for a walk, okay?"

"That's fine."

Barbary followed Heather into their room. Heather sat cross-legged on her bunk with her chin on her fists. Tears ran down her cheeks, but she had stopped crying.

"Just once you'd think — !"

"It's okay, Heather," Barbary said. "Honest. I can find

my way back down. If you argue, he might get suspicious."
She dug around in the bottom of her duffel bag where she
had hidden the plastic pouches of radiation-preserved cat
food. She stuffed a couple into her pocket.

"I guess," Heather said.

Barbary knew better than to say she was relieved not to
have to argue Heather into staying home. Barbary could
wait for Mick outside the elevator housing without dragging
Heather back into full gravity.

"I'll be back in a while," Barbary said. "With Mick." She
hoped.

A knock startled them. Heather flopped down on her bunk
and pretended to sleep.

"I'm coming," Barbary said.

Yoshi opened the door. He was frowning. Barbary thought,
I didn't stay in here *that* long. Maybe he thinks we're having another fight.

"Barbary, I just got a call from Dr. Velory," Yoshi said.
"She wants to see you in the control center."

"Me?" Barbary said. "Why? What — what's wrong?"

"She didn't say," Yoshi said. "But she did not sound
happy."

Heather abandoned all pretense at sleep. She and Barbary looked at each other. Barbary knew they were both
thinking the same thing: Mick is really in trouble this time.
And so are we.


As they left the apartment, Thea glanced up, said "Have a

123

nice time," and went back to work, without even noticing that no one answered her.

Barbary expected the third degree from Yoshi, but he led her to the control center on the one-g level of the station and never asked a single question or made a single accusation. Nor did he prevent Heather from coming along.

Barbary's heart pounded. She walked plus-spin along the empty hallway outside the control center, Heather on her left and Yoshi on her right. They meant her to know they supported her, but instead she felt as if they were the guards marching her to jail. It was just as well they were with her, though, because otherwise she might have turned and run. On the space station, there was no place to run to.

They stopped in the doorway of the control chamber.

Instruments and gauges and consoles and computer displays filled the large room. But all the people who should have been keeping track of the station clustered around a central console. Only Jeanne Velory remained apart. Leaning against another console, her arms folded, she glared at the controllers, who were all making the sorts of sappy noises that adults make when someone shows them a new baby.

"You wanted to see us, Jeanne?" Yoshi said.

She turned slowly toward them. She looked very angry.

"I wanted to see Barbary," she said in a level tone. "I think perhaps she has some explanation for this."

"For what?" Barbary said.

"Will everybody get back to work!" Jeanne shouted.

"Oh, Jeanne, come on," one of the techs said.

"Right now!"

The techs reluctantly broke up their gathering.

Mick lay sprawled on the warm console, licking one front paw and pretending he was not the center of attention. When the last technician had stroked him and returned to work, Mick gazed at Barbary and blinked his eyes.

"For this," Jeanne said.

For an instant Barbary wondered if she could get away with pretending she had not brought him to the station. But if she lied now, even if she got away with it, she would have to keep pretending Mick was not hers. She might stay out of trouble, but he would be sent back to earth, or locked up, or killed, and she would have lost the right to stand up for him.

"Yeah," she said.

"Come with me."

Barbary gathered Mickey in her arms and followed Jeanne.

In her office, Jeanne motioned Barbary to a chair. Behind her desk, the director of the science station became even more imposing than usual.

"This explains your behavior," she said. "But it doesn't explain why you brought a cat with you in the first place, or how you thought you could get away with it."

Barbary huddled in her jacket, holding Mick close.

"What are you going to do to us?" she asked.

"For the time being, the cat will have to stay in one of the labs. They can find a cage big enough for him —"

"A cage! Mick's never been in a cage! He'll go nuts! He'll yowl all the time and drive everybody crazy and they'll get mad and hit him!"

"And you'll have to consider yourself on probation. When things calm down I may be able to arrange for your cat to go back to earth."

"He doesn't have any place to go on earth!" Barbary wailed.

"You'd better put your mind to finding him one," Jeanne said. "That's the best I can do for now."

"But you're the boss here! You can do anything you want. Why can't you just let him stay?"

"Try to understand my position, Barbary. I'm the boss, yes. But everything is complicated right now. I'm still feeling my way, and I'm having to do it while I'm under a microscope. The station has enemies who take every chance they can get to attack it, to cut its funding before it has a chance to prove its worth. One of the things they call it is an expensive toy. So we have to be on particular guard against doing frivolous things —"

"I don't see where a cat is so frivolous," Barbary said belligerently. "Cats can be really useful."

"— or breaking the rules."

Barbary shut her eyes tight.

"Please don't cry."

"I'm not," Barbary whispered.

Jeanne gazed at Barbary. Finally she left her desk and sat in the chair beside Barbary, hitching it around so they faced each other.

"I'm not omnipotent, and some things I just can't explain to you. For the time being, your cat —"

"His name's Mickey!"

"— will have to stay locked up."

"In my room? I won't let him loose, honest."

126

"But he got loose today, didn't he?"

Barbary stared at Mick, who purred in her arms. At least he was all right. The elevator had not crushed him and the cables had not electrocuted him. Somehow he had climbed out of the shield level and escaped from the elevator shaft. Perhaps the same tech who had left the panel open at the bottom of the shaft had forgotten to close one at the top, too.

"It wasn't —" Barbary stopped. If she defended herself against the charge of being careless with Mick, she would have to admit to being in the shield level. She would have to admit that Heather showed her how to get there. So far, Jeanne had left Heather out of this, which was some luck.

"It wasn't what?" Jeanne said.

"Nothing."

"You don't strike me as being the sort of person who likes practical jokes," Jeanne said.

"Jokes?" Barbary said, confused. She did not like feeling confused, and confused seemed to be the way she felt here most of the time.

"Jokes like smuggling a cat on board a space station."

"It wasn't a joke!" Barbary cried. She hid her face against Mick's side.

"Okay, never mind, take it easy." Jeanne patted Barbary's shoulder awkwardly. "Mickey means a lot to you, doesn't he?"

"Uh-huh," Barbary said without looking up.

"I'll try to think of a way for you to keep him. I can't promise anything, so please don't get your hopes up." She hesitated. "This is hard for me, too," she said. "I earned this job, Barbary. I worked hard for it, and I intend to keep it. But I wasn't the only choice for it by a long shot. There are plenty of people who think someone else should have it, and plenty of people who don't much care who has it, as long as it isn't me, or anybody like me."

"But that's stupid," Barbary said. "Why?"

"Things are better than they used to be. A lot better. But there are still people in power who don't think women in general and women of color in particular have what it takes to run things. All I can do is keep proving myself — and keep pretending I don't know about the people who want me to fail. Sometimes that means . . . I can't do exactly what I want to do exactly when I want to do it. Do you understand what I mean?"

"I guess," Barbary said.

"Okay. Come on. Let's go find a place for Mickey, where he'll be comfortable and safe."

Jeanne put her arm around Barbary's shoulders as they started for the door.

"Jeanne?" Barbary said.

"Hmm?"

"If you have to pretend those other people don't exist . . . why did you tell me about them?"

Jeanne hesitated. "You've wanted to do a lot of things that everybody around you said you couldn't possibly do, but you did them anyway. Right?"

"Yeah."

"That's why."

* *

In the control center, Yoshi waited, looking grim, and Heather seemed about to explode from nervousness.

"So this is what all the mystery was about," Yoshi said.

"We'd better talk," Jeanne said, and took him aside.

Barbary joined Heather.

"Was she really mad?" Heather whispered. "What's going to happen?"

"I don't know yet," Barbary said. "I didn't tell her about — you know —"

"Oh, I don't care about that! What about Mick?"

"He has to be locked up. For a while anyway. At first she said she'd have to send him back to earth. But, I don't know, later on it seemed like maybe she might be able to figure out a way I can keep him." She tried to overhear what Yoshi and Jeanne were saying, but they spoke too softly.

"Nobody knows you knew about him," Barbary said to Heather. "We better let them keep thinking that."

"They'd have to think I'm awful dumb —"

"Can I pet him again?"

Heather shut up as one of the technicians sat on his heels beside them.

"He's not used to different people," Barbary said. "Be careful that he doesn't scratch you."

The tech held out his hand for Mick to sniff, then stroked his head and scratched behind his ears.

"I used to have cats back on earth," he said. "They're about the only thing I miss out here."

Mick stretched and purred and nudged Barbary to let him down. She did. To her surprise, he basked in the attention. Back on earth he ran away from anyone but her.

129

"I'm Charlie," the tech said, extending his free hand for Barbary and Heather to shake. Within a few minutes, half the technicians had returned to fuss over Mick and play with him.

"I wonder if there's any catnip in the gardens," someone said.

"We could send for some seeds if there isn't."

"He doesn't like catnip much," Barbary said. "I gave him some when he was little and he just ignored it."

"He'd probably like it now," Charlie said. "Kittens hardly ever do, but he's about the age where he'll start to find it interesting."

"Come on, Barbary," Jeanne said, from beyond the group of people. "Time to go."

"All right." She picked Mickey up. He twisted, trying to free himself, almost as if he knew that he would not like the next place they went to.

"Oh, *ugh!*"

Everyone turned toward the exclamation.

One of the controllers, behind her console, put her hands on her hips and glared at the floor. She reached down and came up again with something thick and stringy pinched between her thumb and forefinger. She lifted it above the edge of the console.

The skinny tail widened out into the dangling brown body of a very large rat, its bony grayish-pink paws curled up against its fur.

Oh, no, Barbary thought. Somehow Mick got into one of the labs, and he's killed one of the animals. He probably wrecked somebody's experiment.

130

"That's really disgusting, Mollie," Heather said.

"Is it dead?" Charlie asked.

"It's still warm," Mollie said. "But it's very dead." She put it down.

"Barbary —" Jeanne said.

"How was he supposed to know?" Barbary held Mick tighter. "Other places we lived, he was *supposed* to catch rats! He's never been in a lab!"

Everybody in the room looked at her, hardly able to believe that anyone would live in a place where rats ran around loose.

"But that's not a lab rat," Heather said.

"Of course it is," Jeanne said.

"What else could it be?" someone else asked.

"Don't be silly," a third said.

Everyone sounded disgusted at the idea that it might be anything but a lab rat.

"If it isn't a lab rat, Heather —" Jeanne said.

"You high-tech people!" Heather said. "You guys have probably never been anywhere near the lab. But I have, and I know what the lab rats look like. First of all they're white, and they have pink eyes. Also they're about half the size of that one. And their teeth are a lot smaller. Actually they're kind of cute. Which that thing isn't."

"That's for sure," Mollie said. "Excuse me, I'm going to go wash my hands."

"Somebody get a box to put it in," Jeanne said. "We'll take it to the lab and ask if it's from the animal room or not."

\* \*

131

Chang Leigh, the chief biologist, looked at Mick with curiosity, and at the body of the rat with astonishment.

"Quite a menagerie," she said. "What's the story?"

"Is this one of yours?" Jeanne asked.

"Certainly not. Nor can I claim the cat, handsome fellow though he is." She stroked Mick, and he arched his back and purred.

"Are you sure?" Jeanne asked. "There's no way this rat could have escaped from the lab —"

"I was afraid you were going to say that," Leigh said. "You caught this creature loose in the station?"

"As far as we can tell — the cat did, I mean."

"Jeanne, we have troubles."

"I was afraid," Jeanne said, "that *you* were going to say *that.*"


Chang Leigh took Barbary, Jeanne, Heather, and Yoshi on a tour of the animal room, just to reassure them that the rat Mickey caught could not have been one of the lab animals, even if one of them had gotten loose. Heather was right, the lab rats were kind of cute. At first Mick pricked his ears and ruffled his whiskers at the sight of so many animated toys all together in such a convenient spot, but then he seemed to realize just how many of them there were. He huddled in the safety of Barbary's arms.

"Okay," Jeanne said, gazing into a cage of small and undeniably cute rats. "I'm convinced."

They returned to Jeanne's office. Barbary kept quiet, glad to have escaped from the laboratory without having to leave

132

Mick locked up and surrounded by rats. But he was tired of being carried. Barbary let him slip out of her arms. He set out exploring.

"This means the station is infested with rats," Jeanne said.

"That could have been the only one," Leigh said. "But I wouldn't bet on it."

"But how —"

"It was inevitable," Leigh said. "Rats always go along with explorers, no matter how many precautions you take. They're sneaky little bastards. They're perfectly capable of stowing away on a ship and getting to shore before the people do."

"Not on a spaceship," Jeanne said drily.

"Metaphorically speaking. And all it takes is one."

"Don't you mean two?"

"Not if the one is pregnant. Which rats frequently are."

"So what now? Poison?"

"I'm a biologist, not an exterminator," Leigh said. "But poisons are seldom an effective long-term solution. The rats can evolve immunities faster than we can invent stronger poisons. And I'd be very uncomfortable about setting out poisons in a closed ecosystem like ours."

Jeanne tapped her fingers on her desk.

"The quickest solution," Leigh said, "would be to get everybody in one place, seal it off, and let the air out of the rest of the station."

Jeanne groaned. "Quick, maybe, but complicated, even under normal conditions. Right now —" She grimaced. "Besides, it would be *terrible* public relations."

"Then your solution's right here." Leigh gestured toward Mick, who had curled up in the corner for a nap. "He won't

133

wipe them out, but he'll keep them under control. And if he catches quite a few of them, it wouldn't hurt to import a few more cats to keep him company. Manxes are good hunters — though I prefer Abyssinians, myself."

Barbary could hardly believe what she heard. She glanced at Heather, who grinned.

"We're going to have to tighten the shipping precautions," Jeanne said. "Otherwise we're going to end up with cockroaches, too, and who knows what. Any suggestions?"

"I'll think about it, and let you know."

"Thanks, Leigh." Jeanne leaned back in her chair and smiled at Barbary. She looked almost relaxed for the first time since Barbary had met her.

"Well, Barbary," she said. "It looks like Mickey has made up his own excuse to stay on."


Yoshi remained silent all the way to their apartment. By the time they got home, Barbary felt like yelling, Go ahead and do whatever it is you're going to do to punish me!

But, of course, the times she had been punished worst had never been in public.

Mick sensed her nervousness. He twisted, trying to free himself. This only made her hold him more firmly, which in turn made him growl.

Inside the apartment, Barbary let Mick down. He ran across the room, jumped over Thea's camera contraption, and disappeared under a chair. The contraption looked almost finished, but Thea was nowhere in sight.

"Sit down, Heather, Barbary," Yoshi said.

They sat.

"Heather, I assume you knew about Mickey from the beginning."

"Sure I did," Heather said.

"No, she didn't!" Barbary said.

"Barbary!" Heather exclaimed. "I *told* you I'd rather get in trouble than have you try to convince people I'm so dumb that —"

"Okay, okay," Barbary said.

"At least now I understand a lot of what's been going on since you arrived," Yoshi said to Barbary. "And why you were so upset at not having your own room."

"Yeah," Barbary said, feeling more and more glum.

Yoshi sat back in his chair, thoughtfully rubbing one finger across his mustache. It made a soft, bristly sound.

"Have you ever read a book called *Catch-22?*" he asked.

"No."

"The main character is in the military, and he does something that he shouldn't do, but it turns out well. So his bosses have to decide whether to court-martial him and send him to jail, or give him a medal. Does that sound familiar?"

"I guess," Barbary said. "You have to decide between hitting me or not."

"Hitting you!" Yoshi sounded both shocked and appalled. "Hitting doesn't even come into it! No, I was trying to decide whether to send both of you to bed without any dinner . . . or whether to fall off my chair laughing. All in all, I think laughing is the best solution." He grinned. "Getting your cat on board *was* a good trick. It reminds me —" He stopped. "Never mind. For now —"

Just then, Thea padded in from Yoshi's room, rubbing her eyes, her hair tousled.

"Good morning," she said. "Or whatever it is. Anything happen while I was asleep?"

Barbary couldn't help it. She started to laugh. Soon Heather and Yoshi joined in. Trying to talk and laugh at the same time, they managed to explain to Thea, and after a moment she was laughing, too.

# Chapter Ten

That night, Barbary lay in bed. Mick purred beside her. She felt peaceful and happy for the first time since she had arrived on the station.

"Barbary?" Heather said.

"I thought you were asleep," Barbary whispered.

"Unh-uh. I feel kind of tired, but I don't feel like going to sleep."

"Are you sure —" She stopped. Heather would just get annoyed if Barbary asked if she were all right. "Yeah," she said. "It's hard to go to sleep after everything that's happened."

"I think we ought to tell Jeanne about the open panel."

"If we do, we'll have to tell her we were down there."

"Yeah. But, after all — nobody ever told me I *couldn't*, and it isn't dangerous, so there's no reason why I shouldn't, and besides, if there's sloppy stuff like that anywhere else on the station, we all ought to look for it, because it could be dangerous."

"If you think we ought to tell her, then I guess we ought to tell her."

"It's probably lucky for all of us that you brought Mickey," Heather said. "Maybe you saved all our lives."

Within a few minutes she was breathing slowly and regularly in the way Barbary had already learned meant she was sound asleep.

Barbary woke early. Burrowed under her covers, Heather slept. Now that Barbary did not have to worry about Mick's whereabouts every minute, he was, of course, purring right next to her. She petted him and tickled his belly, and he play-fought with her hand.

"Today you get to go to work," she whispered. "You get to go hunting, and if you catch anything they'll keep on liking you. Don't catch all the rats, though, or they won't need us anymore."

Bored with playing, he jumped, bounced from the bunk to the desk to the floor, and stopped to lick his paw.

"Got dirty, huh?" she said, and grinned.

She went to take a shower. In half gravity, the big droplets drifted and spread across her skin. She dressed and padded barefoot into the living room. Heather was curled up on the couch next to Mick.

"Good morning," she said. "I called Jeanne's office and we have an appointment with her at eight."

The door of Yoshi's room was closed. Thea's contraption lay on the floor with a plastic cover thrown over it.

"It looks finished," Heather said. "She must have put the lenses in. The plastic's to keep it all clean."

"There's something you ought to know about cats and keeping stuff clean," Barbary said. "Cats shed."

"Well, I know, and he pisses too, but not on the floor —"

"No, *shed*. His hair falls out and grows back in again. You're always finding cat hair around. We'll have to vacuum, or whatever you do, more often."

Heather looked at Mick with a curious, doubtful expression.

"It's not that bad," Barbary said. "And I brush him, so that helps."

"I don't mind," Heather said. "Only I can't imagine what he'll look like without any hair."

"He doesn't lose all his hair!" Barbary said, trying not to laugh. "Just a little at a time. You can't even tell, except between winter and spring. Then he goes from having heavy fur to less fur. I don't know what he'll do here where there isn't any winter or spring."

"I'm glad he doesn't lose all his fur," Heather said. "It's awfully pretty."

They went for breakfast. Mick followed, delighted to be let out of their room. He bounded sideways like a kitten, slid to a stop, and scampered past them going the other direction. Barbary smiled to see him having so much fun, but the problem with letting him free was that she still worried where he would go and what might happen to him. He might end up in the elevator shaft. She could screw the

139

panel on the shield level into place, but she had no idea how Mick had gotten out of the shaft and into the control center. Somewhere there had to be another hole, or loose panel, or something. She was glad they were going to tell Jeanne about the opening.

Everyone in the cafeteria noticed their arrival. Barbary had been novelty enough, but Mick was a wonder. Most of the people on the station had been here several years. Several said the same thing as the technician in the control center: "I don't miss much about earth, but I do miss having a pet." Barbary began to wonder why no one before her had smuggled one on board.

She and Heather ate toast and fruit while the adults fussed over Mick and brought him milk and bits of fish and generally fawned over him. He took it all as if he had been waiting for everyone to notice that he was completely exceptional. Barbary kept an eye on him, half expecting him to stop lapping his milk and spit and claw at one of the people stroking him.

"I don't get it," she said to Heather. "Back on earth he'd hardly let anybody but me get close enough to touch him. And if they did, he bit them."

"I don't think you need to warn people about him anymore," Heather said. "He could get away if he wanted. I think he likes the attention. Maybe he likes being in space so much he's just calmed down. Or maybe . . ."

"What?"

"Maybe he knows practically everybody likes him here. Did they, back on earth?"

"No," Barbary said. "Not at all. Mostly they thought he

140

was a nuisance and I ought to get rid of him."

"There, see? Nobody thinks that up here. Even if somebody doesn't like cats, they'd probably rather put up with Mick than have a bunch of rodents running around loose."

"I guess you're right."

Just before eight o'clock, they rescued Mick from his admirers and took the elevator down to the control center. Barbary kept glancing at Heather, to be sure the gravity did not adversely affect her.

They knocked on Jeanne's door.

"Come in."

Inside, Jeanne gestured to chairs. The screen of her desk computer flashed with squares overlying squares, each containing its own separate message, each blinking at a different, frantic frequency. She turned her back on them to talk to Barbary and Heather.

"Hi, kids," she said. "What's up?"

Heather began. "We thought we ought to tell you . . ."

A few minutes later, Jeanne put holds on all her urgent messages. She hurried with Heather and Barbary to the shield level. In the dim light on the elevator platform, she sat on her heels and looked at the unfastened panel.

"We came down here so Mick could run around and nobody would see him," Heather said.

"Yeah, and he thinks that's why we're here now, too." Barbary had to wrap her arms around him to keep him from running off across the hillocks.

"And we think he climbed in there and that's how he got to the control center — but we don't know where he came out. And he couldn't have opened it himself, could he?"

141

"I don't see how. I don't think it's ever been closed," Jeanne said. "It doesn't look to me like the panel's ever been screwed shut. I guess that's better than if it had somehow come loose by itself, which might mean the whole station was falling apart around us."

She gazed across the hillocks.

"Quite a place," she said. "I've never been here before."

"Barbary suggested we should plant grass and things. Wouldn't that be neat? It'd be like the gardens, only big enough to walk in."

"It would be quite an undertaking — but it might be possible. I'll look into it. After all the excitement has died down. That *is* a good idea, Barbary."

"Thanks," Barbary said. "But could we go now? Mick's getting crazy, and if I let him go I'm afraid he'll find another hole to crawl into."

"Sure."

They returned to Jeanne's office.

"I'm going to call the techs and the mechanics in off the observation platform and put them to work checking the structural integrity of the station," Jeanne said when she had closed the door. "But we've got a lot of grounders here, and I don't want them to panic."

"So don't tell anybody, right?" Heather said.

"Don't go out of your way to spread it around," Jeanne replied. "Everybody who lives here will know within a couple of hours. But even in a crisis we can't evacuate anyone till the station's near perigee — they knew that when they came on board. What we can do is try to maintain some normality while we check out the station. Okay?"

142

"Okay."

"I'm sorry we caused you all this trouble," Barbary said.

"It's all right, Barbary," Jeanne said. "Honestly. Discovering that the station has rats, and that it's had no thorough inspections in the whole time it's been up here aren't things I'd've chosen to happen. But it's better to know about the problems and fix them. We all should be very grateful to you and Heather — and to Mickey."

"Okay."

"Has he caught any more rats?"

"No. But I haven't had that much chance to let him loose. I'm kind of scared that he'll get lost in the elevator again."

"I've been thinking about how to keep track of him. Would he wear a collar, do you think?"

"He did before — he had to have a license. He didn't seem to mind it too much."

Jeanne gave Barbary a piece of elastic with a plastic-encased electronic chip glued to it.

"This is makeshift, but it ought to work. It's a transmitter. We put them on servomechs, and on tools that we use outside. The computer tracks them."

"I'll show you," Heather said.

"Great," Barbary said. She would be happier knowing where Mick was, and he would be happier not being followed around all the time.

She tied the elastic around Mick's neck. He flattened his ears, but he soon grew resigned to the light collar and ignored it.

* *

143

When Barbary and Heather returned to the apartment, it was empty except for Thea's contraption. A long tube secured a camera and several other instruments; sensor wires led from the tube to a microprocessor, which Heather said would connect to the raft's radio and transmit data to the station.

Yoshi had left them a note on the computer — on a piece of paper taped to the terminal. His handwriting was clear and elegant.

"Lessons," the note said. "Rest." And finally, "I am in the library."

Heather sighed. "Vacation's over, I guess. Oh, well, lessons are kind of fun."

Mick prowled around the room, pausing now and then at the door to the outside corridor, but Barbary was not quite ready to let him out into the station. She decided to wait till Heather showed her how to follow the signal on his collar.

Heather introduced Barbary to the computer. They each had a terminal which contained a great deal of built-in information, and which would also call up the station's main library banks and look for whatever it did not have.

"If you can get all that right here," Barbary asked, "why did Yoshi go to the library?"

"To write," Heather said. "He went to the book library, not the computer library. A lot of people brought books from earth because they like to read that way instead of on the computer. I don't understand why myself. But that's how it is. Some of them got together and put their books all

144

in one place so they'd have a library. Anybody can borrow the books. Yoshi likes to work up there."

"What does he do?"

"He's a poet."

"Oh. I mean what does he really do?"

"He really is a poet!" Heather said. "People are, you know."

"Okay, okay, I just never heard of a poet on a space station before."

"I guess maybe you haven't heard of everything in the whole universe yet, then, have you?"

"What are you so mad about?"

"How would you feel if you did something important — something nobody else could do — and somebody said, 'Oh, that's nice, but what do you really do?' "

"I'd be mad," Barbary admitted.

"Well."

"Um, I'm sorry," Barbary said. "Can anybody read one of his poems?"

"You can read everything he's published. It's in the library."

"The computer library?"

"No, the book library."

"Why isn't it in the computer?"

"Yoshi doesn't like computers much."

"Oh." She could think of several questions, but she was afraid she might upset Heather again, so for the moment she kept her silence. Besides, Heather turned on the two terminals and began to show her how to use hers. Almost everyone had computers on earth, so Barbary knew something about them. But it seemed to her that they always judged and graded her and reported her failures to adults.

"I won't hang over your shoulder," Heather said. "But I'll be right here if you need to ask anything." She set both terminals to respond on the screen, rather than by speaking, so she and Barbary could work without interfering with each other.

"Okay."

Heather perched cross-legged on a chair and immersed herself in her own work.

Barbary's computer was smarter than any other she had ever met. And though it acted friendly, it knew a great deal about her. All her records were in memory somewhere, and while she supposed she should not care if a computer had read them, she hoped Heather had not done so. She asked the machine if anybody could read anyone else's records.

It scrolled its reply on the screen. "No, that requires special permission."

Barbary felt relieved. She was not very adept at schoolwork.

The computer chatted with her. It never forgot anything she told it, and it never made fun of her for forgetting things it told to her.

But Barbary realized that it was doing what computers always did. She stood and pushed away the keyboard. In the low gravity her chair tumbled over backward and bounced across the room.

Heather blinked at her, far away.

"What's the matter?"

"This thing is testing me."

Heather looked confused for a moment. "I guess you could

146

call it that. It's finding out what you know so it can tailor lessons for you."

"That's what people always say it's doing, but what they mean is, it's testing you. Why didn't you tell me?"

"I didn't think of it that way. But even if I did, I probably wouldn't have thought to say so — why are you so upset? All the teaching computers I ever heard of work like this."

"I don't like to be tested — I particularly don't like to be tested when I don't know I'm being tested." She recalled one time in particular, when she had been judged by people hidden behind a one-way mirror. Without talking to her, they had decided that she had to go to a different foster family. She "was not adjusting well," whatever that meant. The original family was easier to live with, and a lot more fun, than most of the people she had stayed with. No one, not even the family, ever could or would explain why she had to leave. She had been moved around so often that she would have been glad to stay in a difficult place if she just did not have to move again. But the juvenile authority said she must move; so she moved.

"It's just trying to help you, Barbary."

"Uh-huh. I've heard that before."

"What did it say that made you so mad?"

"I just don't like being tested and graded all the time! I thought maybe here things would be different."

"But it isn't grading you."

"Then why's it doing what it's doing?"

"It needs to find out what you know already about different subjects. Otherwise it'd have to start from the beginning on everything, which would drive you crazy, it'd be so boring, or it'd have to say, Oh, she's twelve, she ought to be *here* — but nobody is ever right on the average for their age in everything, so it would be behind you or ahead of you, and you wouldn't like that either."

"But it will tell everybody what I'm behind on, and they'll say I'm stupid."

"Stupid! Anybody who thinks you're stupid *is* stupid!"

Barbary glared at the floor with her fists clenched.

"Hey, Barbary," Heather said.

"Yeah."

"You can trust me. Honest."

Barbary raised her head. The screen glowed as the patient computer waited for a reply, now and then scrolling out a line of encouragement or a hint. The letters blurred and Barbary blinked them back into focus.

"I'm trying," she whispered. "I guess it must not seem like it. But I am."

Heather hopped off her chair, came around the edge of the computer table, and hugged her hard.

"It's okay," she said. "It's going to be okay."


Once Barbary knew the computer would not report on her to some social worker, she began to enjoy working with it. The time passed so fast she hardly noticed it.

She squeezed her eyes shut, opened them, and looked at the computer screen again. She still had trouble bringing the letters into focus, and she wondered what was wrong. Finished with his prowling, Mick curled near her, purring. For a while he tried to catch the cursor with his paw, but after batting at it a few times, he recognized the glass screen as some weird kind of window and gave up trying to catch the little moving light behind it.

"Hey, Heather, do you have any aspirin?"

Heather glanced up from her own work.

"Sure. What's wrong?"

"My eyes kind of hurt. I never worked on a computer this long before."

"Really? This isn't very long at all."

She followed Heather into the bathroom and found out where they kept the aspirin. Barbary gulped a couple down.

"You ought to rest your eyes in between staring at the screen," Heather said. "Like if you're thinking about how you want to write something, you should close your eyes, or look at something way on the other side of the room."

"Oh. Okay."

"That way you can keep going about as long as you want."

Barbary hoped she would not have to spend all day every day at the computer. Heather had been engrossed in whatever she was doing. It was probably so far ahead of whatever Barbary knew that Barbary would not even be able to understand an explanation, much less the subject.

"Why don't you lie down for a little while?" Heather said. "That'll make the headache go away."

"I will if you will."

"I guess I ought to," Heather said.

When they returned to the living room, Thea had uncovered her contraption.

"Hi, Thea. How's it going?"

"Oh, it's nearly finished," Thea said. "I'm checking the

149

braces, to be sure it'll fit into a raft. I'm going to try it out in a little while."

"Hey, neat," Heather said. "Can we help?"

"There's not that much to do," Thea said. "But sure, you're welcome to come along when I take it out."

Mick strolled over and climbed into her lap.

"Nice kitty," Thea said, scratching him under the chin. "You are a nice kitty, but the last thing I need is cat hair in my lenses."

Thea picked him up and offered him to Barbary, holding him behind the front legs so his paws stuck out in front of him. He bristled his whiskers and looked about to growl. Barbary rescued him.

"We'll take him into our room with us," she said. In a low voice, to Heather, she said, "Pretty soon you better show me how to keep track of him so I can let him out."

"That'll only take a second," Heather said, delighted to have an excuse to put off her afternoon nap a few minutes longer. "Let's do it right now!"

As she headed back to her computer, the call-signal chimed. Heather accepted the message:

"General announcement regarding the alien craft. Main meeting room. Immediately."

"Wow!" Heather said. "Let's go! Thea, did you hear? There's an announcement about the alien ship!"

Thea looked up, frowning and startled.

"An announcement?"

"Yeah, down in the main meeting room. Want to come with us?"

150

Thea hesitated. "No," she said. "I want to finish here. I'll be along later."

"Okay, bye, come on, Barbary!"

Heather headed for the door. Barbary took just enough time to put Mick in the bedroom.

"You be good," she said. "When I come back, you can go out." She hurried after Heather.

# Chapter Eleven

People filled the hallways around the main meeting room. It was even more crowded than the reception for Jeanne. Barbary and Heather ducked around and between people, till they managed to get inside. They could not see anything, even standing on tiptoe, and though most of the adults around them gave them sympathetic looks, the crowd packed the room far too full for anyone to let them nearer the front.

"Thank you for coming."

Jeanne Velory's soft, powerful voice radiated from the speakers.

"Several hours ago, we detected a change in the alien ship's path," Jeanne said. "The change was the result of a deliberate application of acceleration." She paused. "Soon thereafter, we received a radio transmission."

The silence crumbled into chaos. Barbary imagined Jeanne at the front of the room, quiet and patient, not trying to speak above the clamor or shout anyone down, just waiting until the crowd fell silent.

"A transmission!" Heather shouted. "Holy cats, it's aliens! Can you believe it?"

"She hasn't said what it is we're supposed to be believing, yet," Barbary said.

Five minutes passed before the chaos settled enough for Jeanne to speak.

"The transmission is quite simple. It arrived in a large number of languages."

She turned on a recording, and the words flowed over the crowd. Barbary did not understand the first language, nor the second, but quite a few other people did, because they began to murmur to each other.

The crystalline clarity of the voice made Barbary want to sob. She did not know why, except that it was the most beautiful thing she had ever heard in her life.

"Greetings," it said, when it began speaking in English. "We come in peace to welcome you into civilization. Please do not approach us, but wait for our arrival."

It changed languages still again. The voice's beauty continued to increase, as if it were singing.

When the final translation ended, some of the people in the room were crying. Barbary let out the breath she had been holding.

"The alien ship has begun to decelerate," Jeanne said, "at a rate that would be difficult for our technology to match or for humans to tolerate. It will not, as we previously believed, cross the earth's orbit and pass us at high speed. Instead, if it continues decelerating, it will reach zero relative velocity a few thousand kilometers from Atlantis."

The noise of everybody trying to speak made Barbary feel

153

as if she were standing beside a buzz saw. Heather said something, an excited expression on her face, but Barbary could not hear her.

Barbary thought, But it could be an automatic response the alien ship gives every time it comes across some half-civilized bunch of people, like us, who've barely even made it into space.

And then she wondered, How could anything so beautiful be a voice from a machine?

Finally she thought, They're aliens, they can travel to the stars. They can do anything.

The noise level dropped as people began to recover from the first shock of the communication. Barbary began to be able to pick out individual conversations and questions. Everyone was excited, but some were excited with joy, and others with fear. People discussed what the aliens might teach to human beings, or what harm they might cause. She heard several people quote a famous writer, whose theory was that any civilization so advanced it can travel to other stars ought to be too civilized to wage war; and she heard others reply "Hogwash!"

Heather touched Barbary's arm. Barbary turned toward her sister.

Heather was very pale. Barbary grabbed her arm, afraid she might faint and be trampled. Barbary held her up, not absolutely sure that was what Heather wanted, but willing to risk her sister's anger if she was mistaken. Barbary thought Heather was leaning on her, but she was so light that it was hard to tell. Barbary bent down, straining to hear.

"Can we get out of here, do you think?"

"I don't know," Barbary said. "But I'll try."

Supporting Heather, Barbary sidled through the crowd. People tried to make way for her, when they noticed her, but most of them remained deep in conversation. Suddenly the whole room quieted. Barbary spied a space and hurried through it before it disappeared. She only had to go about five more meters to reach the door. She wished the meeting were being held in zero g so she could sly around and between all the people in her way. She kept glancing at her sister. Heather gripped Barbary's arm tight.

The meeting hall fell silent.

"Colleagues," said the secretary-general of the United Nations, her voice a papery whisper. Her presence was so powerful that Barbary could feel it without even being able to see her, and everyone remained so quiet that they seemed to stop breathing.

Barbary plunged through the doorway, pulling Heather along behind her. Sweat ran down her face. She gasped a breath of the cooler air. Ambassador Begay was still speaking, but out here Barbary could only make out her voice, not her words.

"Are you okay?" she asked Heather.

Heather leaned against the wall.

"I think so," she said. "Thanks for getting me out of there."

"You're welcome. I'm kind of glad to be outside, too. Want to go home?"

"I think I better."

They trudged up the corridor, boarded the elevator, and rode to the half-g level.

"Did you see Yoshi anyplace?"

155

"Unh-uh," Barbary said.

"I guess he must still be in the library. When he's writing he sometimes doesn't even hear PA announcements." Back in their home territory, Heather regained her strength. She grinned. "That means we'll probably get to tell him about the aliens."

They reached the apartment and went inside.

"I really am going to take a nap this time," Heather said. "Wake me up when Yoshi gets back so we can both tell him, okay?"

"Sure."

Heather disappeared into her bedroom.

This was the first time Barbary had been by herself with nothing specific to do since she reached Atlantis. The living room seemed large and empty — strange, since it had felt so small the first time she saw it. Then she realized why: Thea had taken her contraption away.

Barbary remembered the aliens' message: "Please do not approach us," it had said. Poor Thea — she must be disappointed, after all her work, not to be able to launch her probe.

"Mick!" Barbary called. She did not see him anywhere in the living room. He must be asleep on the bunk. She crept into the bedroom, hoping not to wake Heather. She chinned herself on the edge of her bed, then climbed the rest of the way to look inside the bookshelves.

No Mick.

Beginning to worry, Barbary leaned over the edge of her bunk. Heather must have fallen asleep as soon as she lay down, because she had not even taken off her shoes or slid under the blanket. But Mick was nowhere to be seen.

Barbary hurried into the living room.

"Mick!"

She hesitated in front of the door to Yoshi's room and knocked. Receiving only silence, she opened it. The sparse furnishing offered no hiding place for a cat.

Thea! Barbary thought. When she moved her contraption, she must have left the door open long enough for Mick to get out. Maybe she thought it was okay for him to go, but more likely she didn't even notice him.

Barbary wanted to curse herself out at the top of her voice. It was her fault, not Thea's, even if Thea had let him out. Barbary should have been more careful. She knew Thea came in and out of the apartment, lost in a fog of plans and calculations, leaving doors open as she passed.

Should she wake Heather? Mick could take care of himself. He would probably come waltzing home in ten minutes, maybe even carrying a big rat that was more or less dead. It was silly to worry about him, now that everyone knew he had permission to be here and a job to do. And Heather looked so tired . . .

The computer could track Mick by his collar. Heather knew how to get the information from the machine, and Barbary did not. But the computer was smart. Perhaps it would understand the question no matter who asked it.

She turned on her terminal and logged in.

Hi, she typed. Do you know where my cat is?

"What is your cat?" the computer said.

Barbary jumped at the sound of the machine's voice. "Can you hear me?" she said.

"I can hear you."

She had forgotten the computer could speak — that it always spoke unless the user turned off the sound.

"My cat — Mick — was in the apartment but now he isn't. He had on a collar with a radio in it. Jeanne said it would tell me where he is in the station."

"I do not understand 'cat,' 'Mick,' or 'collar,' but I do understand 'radio.' Please wait while I obtain more information."

The screen blinked into fancy patterns that changed like a kaleidoscope. After a minute the voice returned.

"I now understand 'cat' and 'collar,' " she said — Barbary thought the voice sounded like a she — "but I cannot discover the meaning of 'Mick.' "

"Mick is the cat's name. It's short for Mickey. Can you find him?"

"The transmitter has not yet been registered, so I am not currently tracking a frequency for Mick, a cat. However, finding an unregistered transmitter is possible. Please wait."

Again the kaleidoscopes appeared. At first the pictures had been beautiful, but now Barbary wished she could make them stop and just get an answer to her question.

Several minutes passed, as the patterns became more colorful, before the voice returned.

"The unregistered transmitter is not in the station."

"But it has to be! Maybe he got out of his collar somehow —"

158

She stopped, realizing that the transmitter would still transmit, even if it were not still attached to Mick.

For a minute Barbary thought she was going to cry. All she could think was that Mick must have gotten himself in such a bad place that his collar had been destroyed.

"Did you look everywhere?" she asked.

"Yes," the computer said. "And I find no unregistered transmitter on the station."

"But you have to!"

"It is outside the station."

"Outside? How could it be outside? Where?"

"The transmission corresponds to the position of a raft that is heading away from the station."

Then Barbary knew what had happened.


Barbary ran down the hall and punched at the controls of the elevator. By the time it arrived, she was about to go looking for the stairs, despite the distance to the hub. When the doors slid open, she plunged inside, still panting. She hit the control for the top level, the nearest to the center, the hub, and grabbed a handhold to steady herself against the tilt.

The elevator halted and she rushed out.

She propelled herself off the floor and into the air. Tumbling and struggling, she managed to grab a strap. She thudded against the wall and bounced to a halt. Here she had no weight, but she still had momentum, and ramming into the wall hurt. When her balance returned, she grabbed the next handhold, and the next, and crawled toward the launch chamber. However much she wanted to run, she would have to move — to sly — smoothly and carefully.

As she was about to enter the raft chamber, she heard voices, arguing. She stopped herself and listened, too desperate even to be embarrassed about eavesdropping.

"I tell you I didn't *know* about the message!" Thea shouted. "If you'd announced it when it first came in — if it weren't for this infernal secrecy —"

"You should have known better," the vice president replied.

"This is a research station, I'm an astronomer. I'm supposed to be doing research."

"It's quite possible that you've committed a diplomatic faux pas in the most important meeting since . . . since . . . the beginning of history!"

"All right, dammit," Thea said. "I've already turned it around. What more do you want?"

Barbary peeked around the doorjamb. The vice president sat in one of the skating chairs that transported novices in free fall. His two bodyguards clung to straps. Thea and Yukiko floated nearby, studying a display.

"Besides," Thea said, grumbling, " 'Please do not approach us'? What the hell does that mean? We *aren't* approaching them. It's just a drone with a camera. If they're so advanced, they can tell it doesn't have any artificial intelligence, and there's nobody in it."

But there is! Barbary thought. Mick's in there — he's got to be!

He must have climbed into Thea's contraption, into the

160

central pipe that formed the basic frame. And he either liked it there too much to leave, or he was too scared or too interested to jump out while Thea carried the contraption to the raft.

"I see you're willing to risk the possibility that the aliens will consider your 'experiment' hostile," the vice president said. "I'm sure your colleagues will be happy to know you're so cavalier about their lives."

"I *told* you I'm bringing it back!"

Barbary let out her breath. Maybe it would be all right. The raft would turn before the aliens decided to shoot it, and Mick would be in the station again long before the raft ran out of air.

"We'll have to broadcast an explanation and an apology," the vice president said. "And you'd better prepare yourself for a disciplinary hearing."

"*You* can't discipline me!" Thea said. "I'm a citizen."

"We'll see." He paused. "How long before the craft returns to the station?"

"It's only been out forty-five minutes," Thea said. "It'll take about an hour to decelerate, turn, and come back. Since I don't have to conserve its fuel anymore."

"Thea . . ." Yukiko said, "it isn't responding."

"*What?*"

Barbary clenched her fists around the handhold.

It *has* to come back! she thought. It *has* to!

"It *has* to be responding," Thea said, with equal desperation.

"It isn't. It's still accelerating."

After a long silence, during which Barbary was afraid to

sneak a look inside the launch chamber, Thea said, "You're right."

In the intense quiet, Barbary could hear her own heart pounding. She bit her lip.

"I'm going to the control chamber," the vice president said. "The military attaché will have to know what's happened. He'll be able to deal with the logistics of destroying the probe."

Barbary froze. The vice president's chair buzzed toward her. If she jumped out in front of him and asked him not to shoot Mickey —

He would probably laugh at her.

If his bodyguards did not shoot *her* for jumping out at him.

She hid in a nearby corridor till he, his bodyguards, and Thea and Yukiko entered the elevator, still arguing.

After they were out of sight, Barbary entered the launch chamber. Heather's raft sat on its tracks, waiting to go out again. Barbary floated to it, opened its door, and slid into the seat.

She stared at the controls. She thought she remembered what Heather had done, but she was not certain. She was not even sure she could figure out in which direction to go to find the alien ship, and Mick's raft. Away from the sun, she guessed. But there was an awful lot of nothing out there, and rafts were awfully small.

Heather said the computer could drive the raft —

She turned it on.

"Can you hear me?"

"I can hear you."

"Do you know where the raft with the transmitter is?"

"Yes."

"I want to go there."

"Please wait."

The kaleidoscope patterns appeared. Barbary gritted her teeth. Computers were supposed to know everything instantly.

But if it knew the location of Mick's raft, why was it making her wait? The only reason she could think of was that it was reporting her.

She slapped the switch that turned off the computer. She did not know if that would keep it from reporting her — if that was what it was doing — but it was the only thing she could think of. She would have to find Mick herself. She pulled down the door and sealed it and tried to remember what control Heather had used first.

"Open up!"

Barbary started at the muffled voice and the rap on the transparent roof.

Heather stared in at her. She looked furious.

Barbary opened the hatch.

"Move over!"

"Heather, they're going to shoot Thea's contraption, and Mick's inside it. I have to stop them —"

"Move over!"

Barbary obeyed.

Heather swung in, slammed the hatch shut, and fastened her seat belt.

"Your computer told me part of it, and I figured out the rest." She took over the controls.

"Thea tried to make her camera come back, but it wouldn't."

"Mick probably knocked loose some of the connections."

Their raft slid into the airlock. The hatch closed.

"I just hope I got here soon enough to get us out," Heather said. "I bet they'll freeze all the hatches in about two seconds, if they haven't already —"

The outer door slid open.

Heather made a sound of triumph and slammed on the power. The acceleration pushed them both back into their seats.

With the raft accelerating and the station growing smaller behind them, Heather glared at Barbary.

"Now," she said. "Why didn't you wake me up?"

"There wasn't time," Barbary said.

"Oh." Heather's scowl softened. "That's a good point."

Barbary squinted into starry space. "How do you know where to go?"

"It's not that hard. From where the station is now, and the direction and speed the ship's approaching, it has to be lined up with Betelgeuse, if Atlantis is directly behind us."

Barbary tried to imagine the geometry of the arrangement Heather described, with all the elements moving independently of one another, and came to the conclusion that it *was* hard, even if Heather was so used to it that she didn't know it.

She peered into the blackness, unable to make out anything but the bright multicolored points of stars.

Heather drew a piece of equipment from the control panel.

164

It looked like a face mask attached to a corrugated rubber pipe. Heather fiddled with a control.

"Here," she said, and pushed the mask toward Barbary. "You can focus with this knob if you need to."

The image of the alien ship floated before her, a sharp, clear three-dimensional miniature, a jumble of spheres and cylinders, panels, struts, and irregularities, some with the hard-edged gleam of metal, some with the softer gloss of plastic, some with a rough and organic appearance, like tree bark. But for all Barbary knew, alien plastic looked like tree bark and their trees looked like steel. If they had trees, or plastic, or steel.

"Can you make it show Mick's raft?"

"That's harder," Heather said, "since I don't know what course Thea used. But I'll try." She bent over the mask, fiddling. "Hey, Barbary," she said.

"Yeah?"

"Were you really going to come out here all by yourself?"

"I guess so. I couldn't think of anything else to do."

"That was brave."

"Dumb, though," Barbary said. She never would have remembered the right controls, and she would have headed off in the wrong direction. "I guess you would have had to come out and get me and Mick both."

"Still, it was brave."

"Did you find Mick yet?" Barbary asked, embarrassed.

"Unh-uh, not yet."

"Can we use his transmitter?"

Heather glanced up, frowning.

"We could," she said, "but we can't, if you see what I mean. We'd have to use the computer, and if we turn it on it would probably lock our controls and take us home. But we'll find him, don't worry."

"Okay," Barbary said. "How long before we catch up to him, do you think?"

"It sort of depends on how fast the raft went out and how rapidly it was accelerating. Which I don't know. But it couldn't have been too fast, or it would use up all its fuel before it got to the ship. Then it wouldn't be able to maneuver, so it would just fly by very fast. Without much time to take pictures. So it has to be going slowly, instead. Anyway, we ought to catch up within a couple of hours. I don't want *us* to run out of fuel — and I don't want to get going so fast that we go right past without seeing Mick."

# Chapter Twelve

The raft hummed through silent space. Barbary kept expecting the stars to change, to appear to grow closer as the raft traveled toward them. But the stars were so distant that she would have to travel for years and years before even a few of them looked any closer or appeared to move, and even then they would still be an enormous distance away.

"Heather . . ."

"Yeah?"

"Thanks for coming with me," she said.

"Hey," Heather said, her cheerfulness touched with bravado. "What are sisters for?"

A red light on the control panel blinked on.

"Uh-oh," Heather said.

"What is it?"

"Radio transmission. Somebody from the station calling us. With orders to come back, probably."

They stared at the light. Heather reached for the radio headset.

167

Barbary grabbed Heather's hand. "If you answer them, they'll just try to persuade us to turn around."

"But we ought to at least tell them that it's us out here," Heather said.

"They probably already know. If they don't, maybe we ought to wait until they figure it out."

"Yoshi will be worried," Heather said sadly, "when he comes home, and he can't find us."

"We're going to have to transmit a message to the aliens anyway," Barbary said. "To tell them we don't mean to bother them, but Mick is in the first raft and we're coming out to rescue him. When we do that, they'll hear us back in Atlantis."

"Uh-huh." Heather gazed into the scanner. "I wonder why they don't want us to come near them? I wonder what they do when somebody does?"

"I guess they could blow us up with death-rays," Barbary said. "But that doesn't seem too civilized."

"And how are we going to explain cats to them? I wonder if they have pets? I wonder what they look like?"

"Maybe they're big cats themselves, like the aliens in *Jenny and the Spaceship*," Barbary said. "Did you read that?"

"Big *cats?*" Heather said. "That's silly, Barbary. The aliens come from some other star system. They evolved on a whole different planet. They probably don't even have the same chemistry we do. They might breathe cyanide or methane or something. Big *cats?*"

"Okay, okay, forget it," Barbary said. "It was just a book."

The radio light continued to glow. To Barbary, it seemed to be getting brighter and brighter, more and more insistent.

Heather finally put on the headset. When she turned on the radio, she spoke before a transmission from Atlantis could come through.

"Raft to alien ship, raft to alien ship. Um . . . hi. My sister Barbary and I — I'm Heather — are trying to rescue a . . . a sort of friend of ours who got stuck in the first raft by mistake. Now we can't make the raft turn around, so we have to catch up to it to get him." She hesitated. "Please don't be mad or anything. Over and out."

In the instant between the time Heather stopped transmitting and turned off the radio, the receiver burst into noise.

"— do you hear me? You girls get back here right now, or —"

Barbary recognized the voice of the vice president.

Heather clicked off the radio.

"He sounded pretty mad," she said. "I guess now they'll tell Yoshi where we are."

"Heather, what if the aliens try to call us? We won't be able to hear them, if we don't leave the radio turned on."

Heather raised one eyebrow and flicked the switch again.

"— return immediately, and you won't be punished. But if —"

She turned it off.

She shrugged cheerfully. "We wouldn't be able to hear the aliens anyway, with Atlantis broadcasting nonstop at us, unless the aliens just blasted through their signal. I'll try later — maybe the vice president will get tired of yelling at us."

"What do we do now?"

"We just wait," Heather said. "I'll keep looking for

169

Mickey's raft. When we find it we'll know better what we need to do and how long it'll take."

"Let me help look," Barbary said.

"Okay."

Heather showed her how to search the star-field for anomalies. At first glance, they looked like stars. But if one looked at an anomaly at two different times, the bright speck would have moved in relation to the real stars. The scanner could save an image and display it alternately with a later view of the same area. An anomaly would blink from one place on the image to another, and the human eye could see the difference. A computer could, too, but it took processing time or a lot of memory, or both, to do what a person could do in an instant.

"Astronomers used to discover new planets and comets and things this way," Heather said. "You can also search by turning up the magnification, but that means you can only see a little bit of space at once. So unless you got really lucky, you'd spend days and days trying to find what you were looking for."

Barbary scanned for the alien ship. When she finally found it she felt pleased with herself, until she remembered how easily Heather had done the same thing.

"Shouldn't Mick's raft be right in between us and the alien ship?" Barbary asked.

"It could be," Heather said. "But it isn't. Nothing moves in straight lines in space, not when there are gravity fields to affect your course. Besides, I'm sure Thea didn't send her camera on a direct line to where the ship is now. She probably planned to arc around it. I mean, she wouldn't want

170

to run into it. There's no way to tell exactly what course she chose. We could call and ask her —"

"As if she'd tell us —"

"She would. But I don't think the VIPs would let her."

"So we just keep looking?"

"Yeah."

Barbary let Heather have the scanner. She knew Heather could find Mick about a hundred times faster than she could.

"What's it like, back on earth?" Heather said abruptly, without looking up. "What's it like to visit a farm, or camp out in the wilderness?" She waited quite a while, as Barbary tried to figure out how to answer her. Finally Heather said in a small voice, "Never mind. I didn't mean to pry."

"It's okay," Barbary said. "It isn't that. It's just a hard question to answer. There are so many different places and different things to see — only I haven't seen most of them. It's hard to get a permit to go out in the wilderness, and you need a lot of equipment, and that costs money. Nobody I knew ever did it."

"What about farms? Did you see cows and horses and stuff?"

"I've never been on a farm, either. There weren't any near where I lived, and they aren't like in movies. They're all automated. Big machines run them. Some of them are covered with plastic to keep the water and the heat in. A couple years ago I snuck off to a zoo. I saw a cow then. It looked kind of bored and dumb. Horses are prettier, but hardly anybody on farms has them anymore. Mostly, rich people keep them to ride."

"How about an ocean?"

"I never saw that, either."

"Oh."

"I wish I could tell you . . ."

"That's all right. I've talked to other people about it, and I've seen pictures and tapes. But I can't figure out what it would be like to see it myself."

"You know, Heather," Barbary said, "an awful lot of people talk about going to the mountains, or going to the ocean, but hardly anybody ever did it. Not anybody I knew, anyway."

"But they could have gone if they wanted."

"Yeah. They could have."

"I usually don't care. But sometimes I wish I could go see the mountains or the ocean, or blue sky."

"Your sky is prettier."

"I bet a blue one would be easier to find a raft in." Heather raised her head from the scanner. She looked exhausted. She had dark circles under her eyes. Barbary felt afraid for her.

"Want me to look?" Barbary asked.

"I'll do it a while longer, then it'll be your turn," Heather said. She stretched, and hunched and relaxed her shoulders a couple of times. "I don't suppose you brought along any sandwiches or anything, did you?"

"No," Barbary said. "I didn't even think of it."

"Oh, well. There are some rations in the survival ball. But they're pretty boring. Probably we should wait till we're really hungry before we use them."

Barbary thought she would get sick if she tried to eat. She felt empty and scared.

172

Heather bent over the scanner once more. "Hey! Look at this!"

Barbary peered into the scanner.

"I just see stars."

"Keep looking." Heather touched the blink control.

In the center of the picture, one of the bright points jumped.

"Is that Mick?"

"Has to be," Heather said.

Barbary flashed the control again; again the image jumped.

"Now zoom in."

Barbary did so. The raft appeared. The airless distance of space transmitted details sharp and clear, but all she could find was the silver and plastic shape of the raft, and the shadows of Thea's contraption inside. Nothing moved.

"There it is!" she said. She magnified it even more. "I don't see Mick, though."

"Let me look."

Heather teased the scanner controls.

"Can you see him?"

"Umm . . . no," Heather said. "I can't. But there's a lot of stuff in there. He'd practically have to sit on top of it for me to find him."

"He's probably sitting *under* it," Barbary said. "Yowling. Or growling like a wildcat."

Heather laughed. "I bet you're right."

Barbary felt both overjoyed and terrified. Heather had found Mick — but Barbary would not be able to stop worrying till she saw for herself that he was all right.

"Where is he?" she asked. "Right in front of us?"

"No, he's kind of over to the side." Heather pointed. "Thea must have planned to circle all the way around the alien ship, then follow it as far as she could. I'm going to have to turn us pretty hard. Are you strapped in?"

"Uh-huh. How long will it take to get there?"

"A couple of hours, maybe. I'm just guessing, though."

"How do we get him when we get there?"

"We can't. There's no safe way to open a raft in space unless everybody inside is in a space suit or a survival ball, and Mick couldn't get in one by himself. So we'll stick out our claws and grab his raft and turn us both around, and go back."

"Oh," Barbary said. She had been hoping there was some way of getting from one raft to another. But at least she would be able to look inside and see Mick.

"Hang on."

The raft plunged into free fall as Heather cut the acceleration. Barbary flung her hands out before her, for it really did feel as if she were falling. The steering rocket flared on, the stars swung, and the rocket on the other side counteracted their spin. Now, Barbary knew, they were traveling in the same direction as before, but Heather had turned the raft a few degrees to the left.

Heather applied some thrust to the raft. The new acceleration would add to their previous velocity, changing their direction and speed so they would be heading more nearly toward Mickey.

Getting to the right spot in space took a lot of care and calculation. It would have been much easier if they could have flown the raft like an airplane, or like a spaceship in a

174

movie, banking into turns and *swooshing* from place to place. But in a vacuum, without any air, ships could not bank into turns or *swoosh*.

"I don't want to kill any more velocity than I have to," Heather said. "It takes too much fuel. So I'll probably have to correct our course a bunch of times. But for now we're sort of heading for where Mick ought to be when we get there."

Barbary tried to figure out how that worked. It sounded suspiciously like a math word problem, which she had never been very good at. She had never seen the point of figuring out when two trains would pass each other when the only trains left were tourist attractions that she had never ridden anyway. But being able to figure out in her head how to meet another raft in space would be useful. She wished she had paid more attention to word problems in school, and she wondered if it was too late for her to learn how to do what Heather could do.

"Hey, Heather — Heather!"

Heather jerked up from the scanner, blinking and confused.

"Huh? What? I'm awake!" She stopped, abashed.

"No, you're not," Barbary said. "You fell asleep sitting up! Heather . . . look . . . maybe . . ." With a shock, she realized how much danger she and Mick had put Heather in.

"Oh, no!" Heather said. "Don't even say it! We're not turning around and going back like we just came out here to make trouble and then lost our nerve!"

Barbary hunched in her seat. She felt miserable.

175

"I'm afraid you're going to get sick," she said.

"I'm okay! I'm just a little tired!" Heather snapped. Her expression softened. "Look," she said. "I don't have to do anything for a while. I could take a nap, and you could keep an eye on the scanner. I'll set it so the image of Mick's raft will get closer and closer to the center till we intercept it. If it goes past the center of the focus, wake me up to correct the course." She showed Barbary the faint band of color outlining a square in the center of the scanner. The other raft lay at the left edge of the screen; it moved, almost imperceptibly, centerward.

"That sounds easy enough," Barbary said.

Heather grinned. "It's a lot easier than trying to sleep in a raft, that's for sure." She squirmed around, trying to get comfortable.

"Lie down crosswise and put your head in my lap," Barbary said. "I'll try not to bonk you with the scanner."

"Okay."

Barbary took off her jacket and tucked it around Heather's shoulders. Heather curled up under it, hiding her eyes from the light of the control panel. Her position still did not look very comfortable, but within a few minutes she was fast asleep.

Barbary looked around.

Far behind her, spinning, lit from behind, the station grew smaller. The earth and the moon each showed only a slender crescent of light, for Barbary was on their night sides. The raft's automatic shield hid the sun and prevented it from blinding her.

Even in the observation bubble of the transport ship, she

176

had never felt so alone and so remote. Beauty surrounded her, a beauty too distant and too enormous for her ever to reach or comprehend. She gazed out at the stars for a very long time, till she realized how long she had been staring. She quickly grabbed the scanner. To her relief, the other raft still lay within the field, halfway to the center of the focus.

Barbary increased the magnification, but that sent the raft all the way off the screen. If she moved the focus, she might not get it back to the place where Heather had aimed it. That also meant she could not use the scanner to find the alien ship, to see if it was doing anything threatening or even simply different.

Heather slept on. The radio receiver's light never flickered from its brilliant red. Trying to keep her attention on the scanner, Barbary forced herself to remain calm. But worry raced through her mind. She began to wonder if perhaps the aliens, and not the space station, might be trying to call the raft: to tell her they understood, everything was all right; to tell her they did not understand, please try to explain more clearly; or to tell her they understood, but they did not believe her and did not trust her and did not care anyway, and were going to shoot both rafts with death-rays.

She put on the headset and turned on the radio and the transmitter.

"This is the second raft calling, in case you didn't hear us before." She whispered, trying not to wake Heather. "We're coming out to rescue the first raft so it won't bother you. It's a mistake that it's out here, and we're really sorry. We're trying to fix things."

177

She turned off the transmitter, leaving the channel open for just a moment.

"Barbary!" Yoshi said. "Is Heather all right?"

"You two turn around and —"

The vice president's voice faded as Barbary cut the power to the radio without replying. She would have liked to reassure Yoshi, but she was afraid to get into a fight with any of the adults, especially Yoshi, or Jeanne if she were there, which she probably was. Jeanne or Yoshi could say things that would make her want to turn around and go back, so they would not be so disappointed with her.

She glanced behind the raft. The science station was a bright turning toy, part lit, part shadowed, spinning between the more distant crescents of the earth and the moon.

Before her, space lay beautiful but still. Somehow the stars reminded her of snow early in the morning, before dawn, in a quiet, windless winter. She peered into the scanner to reassure herself that the other raft was still there. She squinted, searching for any sign of Mick. But his raft drifted onward, showing no signs of life.

She yawned, then shook her head to wake herself up. She could not go to sleep, though Heather's steady breathing in the silence of the little ship had a hypnotic effect. She yawned again. She pinched herself, hard.

A glimmer of light on metal caught her gaze.

Off to the left, far away but as clear as a close-up model, Mick's raft crept along. Now that she had found it, Barbary did not understand how she could have failed to see it for so long. She could tell it was in motion; she could tell her own raft was approaching it, slowly and at a tangent. In the scanner, the image had touched the outer edge of the focus square.

She started to touch Heather's shoulder, but decided against waking her yet. They still had quite a way to go before their raft intercepted Mick's, and Heather needed the rest.

Still careful not to change the direction of the scanner, Barbary increased the magnification. Now she could see part of the raft in the center of the frame. But the transparent roof had not yet come into view. Barbary stared at the image, willing it to move faster so she could look inside. It crept onto the screen, appearing to move sideways because of its orientation and because she was approaching it from behind and to one side. She wished she could see its front. Often, when Mick had ridden in a car, he crouched up front looking through the windshield. But she supposed he would have trouble crouching on the dashboard of a raft, without any gravity.

Something glided through the picture.

Her heart pounding with excitement, Barbary bent closer over the scanner.

"Mick," she whispered, "hey, come past again, okay?" The portion of the image taken up by transparent raft roof increased. She held her breath.

As if he knew she was coming after him, Mick brought himself up short against the plastic and peered directly at her. He opened his mouth wide. If they had not been separated by the vacuum of space, she would have heard his plaintive yowl.

"Okay," she said, laughing with relief. "I'm coming to get you, you dumb cat."

The scanner grew foggy. She had come so close to crying that she had misted up the mask. She sat up and reached into it to rub away the condensation with her sleeve. She glanced outside to check the position of Mick's raft.

To her shock, it — and Mick, looking at her — lay no more than twenty meters away. She was gaining on it.

"Heather!" she cried.

She pushed the scanner out of the way and pulled her jacket off Heather's shoulders. She shook her, but Heather remained sound asleep.

"Heather, come on!"

Barbary did not intend to come this far and lose Mick. She did not know if they could turn around and come back for him if they passed his raft. She jammed her hands into the grasps of the claw controls. She reached out; the grapples extended from beneath the raft. She opened her fingers and closed them; the claws followed her motion.

The distance between the rafts diminished to ten meters, then to five.

Barbary reminded herself again and again that the key to doing anything in space was to do it calmly and smoothly. She did not feel calm. She felt terrified and ignorant. Sweat rolled into her eyes. She could not take her hands from the grasps, and she was afraid to take her gaze off the other raft long enough to lean down and rub her forehead on her sleeve.

"Heather —!"

Even if Heather woke now, there was no time for her to take over the controls. As her raft approached Mick's, so much faster than it had seemed to be moving when they were far away, Barbary grabbed for it.

As she clenched her fingers in the grappler controls, the two rafts came together with a tremendous, wrenching *clang*. Barbary gasped, fearing she had rammed hard enough to breach the hull of Mick's raft or her own. The ships began a slow tumble. Around them, the stars spun. Barbary squeezed her eyes tight shut. That was even worse. She opened her eyes again. The claws kept the two vehicles clamped tight together. She could no longer see Mick, for he was underneath her. But as the reverberations of the crash faded, she heard, transmitted through the hulls, Mick's angry, objecting howl.

She laughed with relief. The motion of the rafts was beginning to make her dizzy, though, and the rafts would continue to tumble till someone used the steering rockets to counteract the spiraling twist. Heather would know how to do it.

"Hey, Heather —"

Usually when Heather wanted to sleep some more, she muttered and pulled her blanket over her head. This time, she lay still.

"Heather?"

Heather's hands felt cold as ice and her skin was very pale. Frightened, Barbary leaned down and put her ear to her sister's chest. Her heartbeat sounded weak and irregular. Barbary wished she knew what it was supposed to sound like, or what it usually sounded like.

Afraid to try to wake her again, Barbary covered her with

her jacket and pillowed Heather's head in her lap.

"It's okay," she said. "I got Mick, I can get us back." She studied the controls. She would have to figure out how to make the ship stop tumbling, then turn it around. She wished she did not feel so dizzy —

Then she thought, You dummy! If you turn on the radio and the computer, back at Atlantis they'll send out the signal to bring us back. It's what they've wanted all along!

She threw the two switches, and got ready to be bawled out.

The radio remained silent.

As the raft rotated, an enormous shape slid past the roof.

The rotation of the raft slowed, though Barbary felt no vibration from the steering rockets.

The huge shape slid into view again, the rotation stopped, and Barbary found herself gazing through the roof at the looming alien ship.

Barbary put her arms across Heather as if she could protect her.

Slowly, the raft moved toward the irregular, multicolored hull.

# Chapter Thirteen

The alien ship drew the raft closer, growing larger and larger till its expanse of incomprehensible shapes stretched as far as Barbary could see.

Trembling, she hugged Heather closer. She wrapped her jacket closer around her sister's shoulders, trying to keep her warm. The raft slid between two irregular projections from the alien ship's hull: a spire taller than any building on earth, covered with delicate strands and symbols, and a wavy, faceted shape resembling the crystals that form around a string suspended in a supersaturated solution of sugar and water.

Roof first, Barbary's raft floated toward a wide black slash in the ship's hull. If she did not keep telling herself she was going "up," she felt as if she were falling, upside down and in slow motion.

Intense darkness closed in around her.

The raft's control panel spread a ghostly light on Heather's pale face and Barbary's hands. She heard the echo of Mick's plaintive miaow, and the feathery whisper of Heather's breath.

A faint chime rang, growing louder and closer. Barbary blinked, trying to figure out if she only imagined light outside the raft, or if she were seeing a glow as gentle as dawn. The ringing reached a pleasant level and remained there, while the light brightened till Barbary could see. She had weight as well, but she had not noticed when the gravity appeared. She felt as if she weighed as much as she did on earth, and this increased her concern for Heather.

Her raft hung in a round room whose surface glistened like mother-of-pearl. The columns supporting the ceiling looked like frozen waterfalls or translucent pillars of melted glass. She searched for the opening that had let her in, but it had closed or sealed itself up. From the wind-chime sound transmitted to her through the raft's body, she decided she must be surrounded by an atmosphere, but she did not know if it was oxygen or — as Heather had speculated — methane or cyanide. She had no way to tell whether it was safe to breathe, or poisonous.

Mick miaowed again, louder.

"It's okay, Mick," she said. She swallowed hard, trying to steady her voice. "It's going to be okay."

"Do you hear us?"

The radio spoke with the beautiful voice of the alien's first message to Atlantis.

"Yes," she whispered, her throat dry. "Can you hear me?"

"We sense you. Will you meet us?"

"I want to. I really do," Barbary said. "But I have to get

Heather into zero g and back to the space station. She's sick and I can't wake her up. The gravity's too strong for her here. Besides, all the important people are waiting to meet you, and they'll be really angry if I see you first."

"But," the voice said, "you have already seen us."

Barbary stared around the chamber, looking for creatures, great ugly things like the aliens in old movies, or small furry things like the aliens in books. They must be hiding behind the tall glass pillars.

The gravity faded till it was barely enough to give Barbary's surroundings a "down" and an "up."

"Is this gravity more comfortable for you?"

"Yes," Barbary said. "Thanks."

"We believed we calibrated your gravity correctly."

"You did," Barbary said. "At least it felt okay to me. But Heather . . . Heather has to live in lower gravity. Won't you let us go? She's sick! Anyway, I can't see you —" She stopped, amazed.

Though she had not seen them move, the crystal columns had come closer. They clustered around her. Their rigid forms remained upright, yet they gave the impression of bending down like a group of worried aunts or friendly trees. A long row of crystalline fibers grew along the side of each column. The fibers quivered rapidly, vibrating against and stroking the main body of each being, producing the wind-chime voices.

"Oh," she said. "Oh. I *do* see you. You're beautiful!"

"We will loose your craft if you wish," the voice on the radio said. "But our ship will reach your habitat before your

185

vessel could fly to it, and here the gravity can be controlled."

"Can you hurry? I'm really worried about Heather."

"We will hurry."

Barbary listened to Heather's rapid, irregular heartbeat.

"Can't you help her?" she said to the aliens. She remembered all the movies she had seen where people got hurt and aliens healed them. "Can't you make her well? Aliens are supposed to be able to make people well!"

"But we have only just met you," one of the aliens said, perplexed and regretful. "We know little of your physiology. Perhaps in a few decades, if you wish us to study you . . ."

Barbary thought she should have learned by now not to expect anything to work the way it did in books or movies. She leaned over Heather again, willing her to awaken.

Heather's eyelids fluttered.

"Barbary . . . ?"

Heather opened her eyes. She sounded weak, confused, and tired.

"It's okay, Heather. Anyway, I think it is — what about you?"

"I feel kind of awful. What happened?"

"We're on the alien ship."

A spark of excitement brought some of the color back to her sister's cheeks. She struggled to a sitting position.

"Are there aliens?" Heather whispered. She was shivering. Barbary chafed her cold hands and helped her put on the jacket.

"There are other beings," the gentle voice said. "We hope

186

not to be alien, one to the other, for very long. Will you meet us?"

"Can we breathe your air?" Heather hugged the jacket around her.

"It is not our air. We do not use air. It is your air. You should find it life-sustaining, uninfectious, and sufficiently warm to maintain you."

Barbary gingerly cracked the seal of the roof-hatch. Warm, fresh air filled the raft. Heather took a deep breath. Her shivering eased.

"If you join us," a voice said, no longer from the radio but from one of the crystalline beings, "then we may rotate your vehicles and release the small person in the lower craft. It does not respond to our communications in an intelligible fashion, and it appears to be quite perturbed."

Barbary could not help it: she laughed. Heather managed to smile. Barbary picked her up — her weight was insignificant in this gravity — and carried her from the raft. The aliens made a spot among them for her; they slid across the mother-of-pearl floor as if, like starfish, they had thousands of tiny sucker-feet at their bases. The floor gave off a comforting warmth. Barbary laid Heather on the yielding surface.

"I'm okay, I really am," Heather said. She tried to sit up, but she was still weak. Barbary helped her, letting Heather lean back against her. Heather gazed at the aliens. "Holy cow."

Mick's furry form hurtled across the space between the rafts and Barbary. He landed against her with all four feet extended and stopped himself by hooking his claws into her shirt. Somehow he managed to do it without touching her skin with his claws. He burrowed his head against her, and she wrapped her arms around him and laid her cheek against his soft fur.

"Boy, Mick," she whispered, "did you cause a lot of trouble."

She looked at the beings, who had rotated the rafts and opened the hatch of Mick's with no help from her. They could have opened up her craft and plucked her and Heather out like peas from a pod, if they had wanted to.

"Aren't you mad?" she asked.

"Our psychology differs from what we understand of yours, but we believe you would consider us sane."

"I didn't mean mad-crazy. I meant mad-angry. We didn't mean to bother you, but we had to rescue Mick."

"We comprehend this. We are not mad-angry," the nearest being said. "How could we rouse ourselves to anger over actions taken in distress?"

"Then how come you asked us not to approach you when you first called us?"

"When a species advances beyond a certain point, it must be introduced to civilization. Otherwise it would discover galactic society, and the rules of galactic society, in a random way. This might cause it shock. Yet even when a people has reached a technological position of adequacy, it may not be ready in the psychological sense to meet other beings. We have found, through experience, that meeting new citizens is easier for them if they are in a large group of their own people. Then their fear of other beings, their xenophobia — which is inevitable in some degree — is less acute. In this case, however, we recognized an emergency."

"Hasn't anyone ever approached you before?"

"Yes," the being said. "Several times. But always with the aim of conquest or attack."

"What did you do to them?"

"We showed them the futility of violence. Oftentimes disarming the aggressor is sufficient, though sometimes their aggression must be turned back upon them."

Barbary decided to leave questions on that subject till later. She wondered if she was ready to find out all the things the beings could do if they had to.

But Heather felt braver, despite her pallor.

"What rules did you mean?"

"The rules that, beyond your own planet, you may create, but you may not destroy. You may observe, but you may not interfere."

Those rules sounded reasonable to Barbary. They sounded like what any sensible person would try to do.

"A lot of people won't like those rules," Heather said, her expression troubled. "They'll want to break them."

"They will be persuaded to comply. There is no choice."

Heather leaned against Barbary, thoughtful and solemn. Barbary tried to think of something to say.

Mick changed the subject for her. He had stopped burrowing into her armpit. He curled against her, purring and watching. Now he squirmed out of her arms and leaped into the air, coming down and bouncing ten meters away.

He stalked up to one of the beings and sniffed its base — its feet? — then rubbed against its side. His fur stroking the crystal surface made a electric, musical note. The beings swiveled toward him, fascinated.

"What a delightful feeling!" said the one that Mick had touched. "What a fine song the small person has invented!"

"He's pretty inventive, all right," Barbary said.

"I do not wish to ask a rude question," one of the beings said, "but why is the small person permitted to operate the vehicle? The controls have not been adapted to him."

"Um, that's a long story," Barbary said.

"We love long stories. They help pass the time of travel between the stars."

Heather drew herself back from her troubled reverie. "How long have you been traveling?" she asked.

"About a billion of your years."

"Your people have had space travel for a billion years?"

"Oh, no, we have had space travel for a time an order of magnitude longer: for ten billion of your years. I thought you meant to ask how long we here had been exploring the stars."

"Ten billion years of star travel," Heather said. "You must be the oldest intelligent species in the universe."

"We have not found any older, but we search, and hope."

Heather stared at the beings in awe. "No wonder you like long stories." She tried to smile. "Barbary, you can show them magic tricks."

"Magic? You have begun to use technology, yet you believe in magic?"

"Not real magic, that's just what it's called." Barbary tried to think of a quick way to explain, but gave up. "Um, it's another long story."

"How excellent," the being said. "We will look forward to hearing it."

"I'm Barbary," Barbary said, remembering her manners, "and this is Heather, my sister. And the — the small person is Mickey."

"We do not have names, as you know them," one of the beings said. "Each of us forms impressions of all others, and refers to the individual by the position in the image."

"That sounds complicated," Barbary said.

"Not as complicated as recalling so many individual designations," the crystal being said. "Without a pattern, how do you tell each other apart?"

Barbary, who had been trying to fix in her mind the variations between the beings so she could remember each one's name — if they had had names to tell her — looked over at Heather. They both burst out laughing.

The delicate filaments on each being quivered and twined, and multitudes of wind-chime voices rang. At first Barbary wondered if she had hurt their feelings by laughing, and then she believed the beings were laughing along with her.

"Another ship is approaching," the musical voice said. "The beings within appear to be . . . quite perturbed."

"They don't know what's happened to us," Heather said. "They probably think we've been swallowed up."

"As indeed you have."

"To be eaten, I mean."

191

"Oh, no. We do not ingest organic molecules. Will you speak with them?"

"Can we? Please?" Heather said. "My father will be worried."

"Should we?" Barbary said.

"Of course we should!" Heather said. "What do you mean?"

"Maybe if they worry about us a little more, they won't be so mad at us when we go back."

"If they're going to be mad, they're going to be mad," Heather said. "I don't want Yoshi to be worried anymore — and I don't want anybody out there to do anything that the other beings might think they need to be shown is futile."

"Okay," Barbary said.

"Would you like to speak to them now?"

"Yes, please," Heather said.

"They will hear you."

Barbary saw no radio equipment, no change in the chamber to indicate a transmitter.

"Hi, this is Heather," Heather said to the air.

"Heather!" Yoshi said. "Are you all right? What about Barbary?"

"I'm okay."

"So am I," Barbary said. "And so is Mick."

"What's happening in there?" Jeanne asked.

Barbary looked at Heather, who gazed back at her and smiled.

"We're with the — the beings in the starship," Barbary said. "They're bringing us home."